Toghane,
Thank you for [illegible]
with me on my project
SC Unite, you absoulutely
rocked as Monique Foster!

SIDE CHICKS UNITE, LLC

by

LaShawn Grice

LaShawn Grice
1/5/18

Printed in the United States of America

First Printing, 2015

ISBN: 978-1-62217-475-1

To all the side chicks, you have a place in this world.
I don't care what anyone says.
One love,
Alexis Harrington

Acknowledgments

I WOULD LIKE TO EXPRESS my gratitude to the many people who saw me through this book; to all those who provided support, talked things over, read, offered comments, and assisted in the editing, proofreading and design.

I wish to personally thank the following people: Mary Honey B Morrison for allowing me to join her "write a book in 90 days challenge" without being a part of this group I honestly don't think I would have finished; my daughter Terranique Grice and my sister and BFF Billie Buckner who read, offered comments, and encouraged me to keep writing when I wanted to quit; my son Malvern Kirvin for being you; my mom Bernice Grice; Laugh Your Class Off Family – one love. Ken Lewis for the constant laughter - out of our silliness, I was able to bring a couple characters to life; Everod Vernon for your encouragement, feedback on the cover design through the countless changes, and insight on Caribbean culture; my supervisor Shawanda Freeman and my co-worker Shannon Newton thank you ladies for the friendship, laughter and encouraging me throughout this process.

Last, but not least thank you to all who will read this book I hope you enjoy it! If I forgot anyone, please blame it to my head and not my heart.

ALEXIS

WHY DOES MY CELLPHONE VIBRATE so loud? Who in the hell is texting me at 1:00 am?

Blindly, I searched for my iPhone on the nightstand. My eyes struggled to look at the blurry text.

Sexy, I can't lie to you. I've gotten married. I don't know why. You have no idea how many times I've thought about it. Why? Damn good question. If you know a good answer...please tell me. I laid the phone facedown and it started vibrating, again. *I'm not dealing with this right now.*

If you still want to see me or talk to me just txt or call. Yes, I wanted to see you tonight, but wanting is just that...I slowly typed, congrats! What does he expect me to say? I feel some type of way. We were supposed to get married. Are you mad at me? And congrats are just that, my mind wasn't and isn't in it. I know that's bad to say but I miss me... As I sat up in the bed my fingers couldn't type fast enough. Hell yeah I'm mad. I hurt because we talked about getting married. I never thought you would marry someone else. I hope things work out for you. No, it's not sad to say. You have a right to feel the way you feel. I should have cussed him out and told him to eat out my ass and feed me bacon, but I always take the high road. I should have turned my phone off or ignored his text, but I couldn't.

But I'm sure you don't want to see me again... he texted.

I didn't say that. You will always be my friend.

I hear you but you know what I mean... he replied.

No, what do you mean?

Whatever, but in case you don't...me lying next to you, in you and tasting you...that's it.

Lol...you are married. Why would you want to do those things to me?

Lol, because it was and is great...you really asked me that?

I guess I wasn't that good...

You were great. You know that.

That didn't answer the question though.

I thought I did. I still want to see you, but I won't.

Ok, I want try then...as bad as I would love to see you...like today.

I meant won't try, guess that was wishful thinking...lol

Goodnight Matthew

Goodnight Lexi

After the text marathon with Matthew I could not go back to sleep. Why do I always end up in these types of situationships?

* * *

I was devastated when Matthew texted me at 1:00 am to tell me that he had lied and had already gotten married. He had the nerve to want me to still have sex with him. I wish I would. If I wasn't good enough to marry I am no longer good enough to bed. I am tired of being the other woman. I am not a bad-looking woman. I exercise at least four times a week to maintain my toned 5'8" frame. I mesmerize men with my hazel eyes and wavy auburn shoulder-length hair. I needed to get away from Detroit before I caught a case fooling with Matthew McDonald.

When I got offered a job as a radio personality at LOVE 102 I gladly left my hometown of Detroit, Michigan, to move to Atlanta. Being close to my family is just what I needed, especially my two younger sisters: Aubrey, thirty-five, who we call Bre Bear, and Autumn, the baby of the family, nicknamed Dani - short for her middle name Danielle is thirty-two.

I loved my job at WGPR. I worked the 10:00 am – 3:00 pm slot for five years. This new job is the same time slot that I had in Detroit. It's cool though. I won't be there long; I have plans to change stations and be on the afternoon drive. My goal is to join "The Ride" with Si-Man and Chubb Rock from 3:00 – 7:00 pm. They needed some estrogen to balance out all that testosterone. I look forward to chiming in on the carpool conversation and giving them a mature woman's perspective on controversial topics. All black women are not bitter, mean, or gold-diggers. There are good sisters out here that will ride for her man, support her man, take care of her man, and not bring drama. Not all accomplished sistahs buy into the whole "I'm a strong independent educated black woman, and don't need no man, so hear me roar" bullshit. There are some women who have a lot to add to a relationship and do not define themselves by their title.

One thing I know for sure is that a bad attitude and titles can't protect you, keep you warm at night, or hold you when life has knocked you down. There are actually some women, black women, who understand that it is hard in these streets for a black man, and home is the one place where you always need to have peace. And they strive to provide that. There are black women who are sexy, sensual, and comfortable in their skin and are willing to please their man and don't use sex as a weapon or bargaining tool unless it's all in fun. My motto is, "If you can get it up, I'll get it down."

I'm not a religious person; I am spiritual and believe in a higher power; however, religious doctrine, the whole heaven and hell thing, makes my spirit heavy...miss me with that. I love to meditate, do yoga, and eat as healthily as possible. There are days I will not turn on the TV so I can sit in silence and quiet my mind - that is when you can get in touch with your true self. This move is good. It got me away from Matthew's lying ass before someone got hurt.

As soon I touched down in Atlanta my sisters whisked me away on a seven-day cruise to Ocho Rios, Jamaica and the Grand Cayman Islands. We had a great time. I loved sitting on the twenty-one-and-older part of the Carnival Victory cruise ship. It was an overcast day; the breeze and sound of the waves were calming. I laid in the lounge chair under the cabana listening to old school music, people-watching, and sipping on a blue margarita I noticed people of all shapes, sizes, and nationalities. One thing for sure - swimsuits don't care who wears them. Some of these people need to be wearing blankets. At thirty-seven I'm in pretty good shape, but I would not be caught dead in some of this mess. I'm so glad I came on this cruise. This was just what I needed: a healing for my soul. I needed some alone time to relax, reflect, and to process everything that has happened in the past couple of months. I don't know why I still had the text messages from Matthew. For some reason I couldn't delete them.

Just as the soft crooning sounds of Freddie Jackson's "I Could Use a Little Love (Right Now)" started playing, I heard, "Excuse me most beautiful lady, is this seat taken?" I looked up and Michael, the tall, dark, chocolate-handsome brother I danced with at the club was standing in front of me wearing a white tank top, black Nike basketball trunks, and black Nike flip flops. I wanted to say, "Don't you see all these empty seats? Of course the seat is not taken," but I didn't. I smiled and said, "No." I got a whiff of his cologne as he sat down in the chair next to me and asked, "Why are you sitting here alone? Where are ya sisters?" My body immediately started giving off pheromones. "They're somewhere on the ship" I replied. "You should have called me. I would have accompanied you. I'm in room 2249." My breathing became shallow as my stomach churned. I didn't know what to say. Finally, in a horrible Jamaican accent I said, "Me gon call ya da next time, Mon." The man was so fine and his accent melted my heart. I thought *he can get it.* Besides, what happens in international waters never happened.

AUTUMN

THIS MORNING WAS HELL! I woke up at 3:00 am for no apparent reason. *I wish I was still on the cruise ship.* As I headed toward the bathroom my head started spinning and my stomach felt queasy. I made a detour to the kitchen for a bottle of Dasani water. Water is my cure for everything. I stumbled back to my bed and tossed and turned, trying my best to fall back asleep. The clock on my nightstand read five o'clock, only an hour before I would have to get up, get dressed, and report to Sodom and Gomorrah. Damn, I hated this job and this sleepless routine on Sunday night was starting to take its toll. When the alarm went off at six, I hit snooze as usual, I contemplated if I should call out sick. I should have followed my dream of becoming an actress, but I listened to my mother and went to college. I wanted to major in theatre, but my mother was not having it. "I will not pay for you to waste your time in theatre. What are you going to do when you graduate? Are you going to be a waitress while you wait for auditions? Do you think you can get around in this world off your looks?" I was pissed. My older sister Aubrey could use her looks to model, but I had to get a college degree. I was 5'7" – an inch shorter than Alexis - and had the same color hazel eyes and hair color; unlike her I wore my hair in a variety of hairstyles. After my first year of college I dropped out and joined the Army. When I got pregnant, with my daughter Morgan, my mother was fuming.

After much-needed prayer I was able to get out of bed and take my Synthroid and vitamin B-12. I turned on the shower so the water could get hot while I brushed my teeth. When I stepped out of the shower I felt like I could face the day and deal with the traffic on I-85N. I rubbed my concoction of coconut oil and shea butter over my body and then put on some Energy lotion from Bath & Body Works. I'm not sure if it gave me energy, but I loved the mango scent.

I hope Morgan is dressed. This is the first day of school for Fulton County and she doesn't need to miss the bus. "Morgan, are you dressed?" I shouted.

"Almost."

"Let's go! I am not dealing with your slowness this school year."

"Mom, I'm almost ready. Relax. I'm trying to get my hair right."

"Relax hell! I could have combed your hair and we could be out the door by now." I'm trying to let her grow up and do her own hair, but if she keeps this up I will put some ponytails and barrettes in it and keep it moving. Most of these kids look too grown anyway.

The partly cloudy day matched my spirit. The traffic was horrendous, which is normal for the first day of school in Fulton County. I-85N was a parking lot due to an accident and although it was off to the side of the road traffic was still backed up because of nosy people looking instead of driving and focusing on their own destinations. My soul walked away as soon as I walked into my office. No amount of energy lotion would bring it back. Today is the first day of Oprah and Deepak's twenty-one-day meditation. There's got to be a better way to make a living. There's got to be more to life than this. I felt melancholy. Maybe because it's close to the anniversary of the day I was attacked when I was on deployment. It has been eight years and I still get depressed. The scars are a constant reminder. I rubbed the scar on my left cheek this morning and thought *will I ever get over this?*

I will never forget that day. The day started off uneventfully, until an argument with Tony would change the course of my day and my life. He used to be in the military, so I don't understand how he could forget that when you're deployed it's hard being away from your family and friends.

A lot of times when I called home he didn't answer the phone and when he did he acted like he didn't have time to talk. We got into an argument and I decided exercise to blow off some steam. I went downstairs to the hotel's fitness center. The keypad to the fitness center door was missing, so it was propped open. No big deal, I thought as I climbed onto the elliptical machine. I was listening to my jam by Mary J. Blige, "Be Without You." I should have followed my mind and closed the door so I could sing off key, but I didn't. Suddenly a Hispanic male came running in. *He must think he's Rocky out here running in one-hundred-plus degree weather,* I thought. And he did. He punched me twice in the right side of my body and hit me in the face. I stopped mid-glide and started hitting him back. I grabbed him by the corner of his shirt and yanked as hard as I could. He fell in front of me and I kept punching him while hollering for help. No one ever came. He finally ran out of the room and I grabbed my cellphone and ran out of the room too. I was confused, scared, and didn't know what to do or which way to go. By the time someone showed up I was hysterical. I kept screaming that this guy came in and hit me. I had no idea I had been cut until I felt blood ooze down my face and neck. I panicked. I remember people rushing to put towels and maxi pads on top of my head. Everything was a blur; I remember Sergeant Coleman telling me to open my eyes. When I got to the hospital I had been cut several times in the top of my head, face, arm, and stomach. My hair was matted from the blood. All the skin was gone from my left elbow. Although the scars have healed physically, mentally I am a wreck. I constantly battle with depression, insomnia, and suicidal thoughts. It is hard to maintain a romantic relationship or any other kind of relationship. Sometimes I just don't want to be around anyone. PTSD is real.

AUBREY

My hands look old for 35 years. They definitely don't match the rest of my body. The deep ridges reveal hands that are no longer soft like they were when I modeled. I was in demand as an African-American Supermodel. At 5'10" I weighed one hundred and ten pounds soaking wet. Both my sisters have hazel eyes like my mother, but I have green eyes like my father. We all share the same caramel skin color and wavy auburn hair. Since I started my interior design company, Distinctive Designs by Aubrey, I am no stranger to manual labor. I have paid my dues and now I am one of the most sought-after interior designers in Atlanta. I love what I do and I have a line of novice designers waiting for the chance to work for me. I no longer have to lift a picture frame, hold a hammer, or nail unless I want. However, there are still some things I prefer to do myself. I have always like decorating. As a child I would rearrange my bedroom furniture and posters on my bedroom walls monthly. Daddy used to say, "Don't you ever marry a blind man because you move the furniture around too much and the poor man will fuck around and kill himself 'cause you moved the couch." I would laugh. Probably because I knew it was true.

I officially fell in love with interior design in the eleventh grade. Although I was apprehensive about the class because I can't draw stick people, I took interior design as an elective. I loved collecting carpet samples and fabric swatches - the feel of it all excited me. I would spend hours cutting pictures out of magazines and creating room designs. I have dabbled in other careers, but never felt fulfilled until I decided to pursue my first love which is decorating and de-cluttering. I can honestly say can't nobody clean like me. I absolutely love cleaning. I have been called lightweight OCD. I've heard that cleanliness is next to godliness. Lord knows I'm not a saint; as a matter of fact I straddle the fence. I probably need to jump over to hell's highway.

I have a beautiful life. I am married to a fine successful black man with a heart of gold and he treats me like a queen. I only work because I love what I do, not because I have to help make ends meet. Kai works as a sports manager and he is the Bishop of New Vision International Worship Cathedral. Kai is handsome; he is 6'1", has dark brown eyes, a muscular build, and a Colgate smile. He is forty, but does not look a day over thirty-five. He is everything any woman would want in a man. Yet, I feel like something is missing. I mean, we live in Alpharetta in a $600,000 house. We have an adorable nine-month- old son, KJ - short for Kai Jr. He is the spitting image of his father. He is our miracle child; it was hard to get pregnant. I was diagnosed with polycystic ovarian syndrome when I was twenty-six, and the doctor told me that it would be difficult for me to have kids if I had any at all. Yes, we have a near- perfect life, except for our sex life. Kai and I are like oil and water in the bedroom. He only likes two positions - missionary or me on top of him. I can't even do tricks while I'm riding. He always pulls me close; he says he likes the closeness. I am all for closeness, but I need to take a walk on the wild side every now and then. I am open to trying anything once. I just wish Kai was. Oh well, sometimes if you can't eat what you want at home, you have to eat out.

KAI

Good morning sleeping beauty; have a beautiful day, I texted.

Good morning, honey, you too, Bre replied.

I love my green-eyed, honey-brown-skinned wife. She is beautiful inside and out, but she can be a time bomb. At times, I affectionately call her TNT; it doesn't take much to set her off. I was happy she was able to do a girls' trip with her sisters. She seems a lot calmer since she returned from the cruise. Bre is the middle child and suffers from the Jan Brady syndrome; she always feels like she has to prove herself, so she is quite the perfectionist and a neat freak. Nothing, I mean nothing, can ever be out of place. The bed has to be made as soon as we get out of it. If I sleep too long I think she would make the bed with me in it. KJ catches hell with his toys and he is not allowed to pull up to the coffee table without getting his hands popped for leaving fingerprints on the glass. He is going to be afraid of furniture. In all her madness I love her. I'm so thankful that my boy Curtis introduced us at his birthday party. When she walked into the room all eyes were on her. She was quiet but oozed confidence. She had a sexiness about her that made both men and women look. Bre is a former supermodel; however, she didn't act stuck-up. She is high-maintenance and independent, but she is not one of those neck-shaking, eyes-rolling, strong, independent "I don't need a man" type of sistahs. She let me know during our first date that although she didn't need a man; she wanted one.

We've been married for five years and we have had our share of problems, but I love this woman with all my heart. She shows me daily how much she appreciates and loves me and our son. My only regret is that I'm not as open in bed as she would like. I know she suppresses her wild side. She is a lady in the streets and can be a freak between the sheets. Before we got married we would have sex anywhere, anytime, or any place. Now that I've been called to preach I don't think it's Godly. I know I don't satisfy her in the bedroom anymore and I hope it does not become too difficult for her and I lose her.

VANESSA

EWWW. I CAN'T STAND CARLOS! He will do for now, since I am temporarily divorce. I'm so tired of pretending to want men when in actuality they disgust me. I only married Derrick so the nosy church folk and my family would stay out of my business and stop asking me when I was getting married. I must have been some kind of fool to marry an ex-convict who had been in federal prison for twenty-five years for drug trafficking and selling cocaine to an undercover federal agent. We'd only been married for 3 months and this ungrateful Negro had the audacity to cheat on me. I'm not a beauty queen, but I look all right. I'm 5'6", fair-skinned I have big boobs but could use a little more junk in my trunk...my butt is flat. If he was going to cheat one would think he would cheat up, but noooo, he cheated with some stripper who worked at the strip club Follies. To make matters worse this tramp has a man. Derrick's dumb ass got into an argument with his side chick's man at the club and he beat him with a bat. When the police arrested him they found a gun and knife in our car. He knew that his ex-felon criminal ass cannot possess a gun. Hail to the power of the "V."

I spent over $50,000 on a wedding to keep up a façade. We got married at Chateau Elan on the Matisse Lawn and the reception was held in the Debussy Ballroom, which was perfect for the 300 guests. It was beautiful. I spared no expenses. There was plenty of food and alcohol. Lord knows I needed hard liquor to deal with the reality of what I'd done. Hell, I needed a hit of meth, crack, or something strong to numb the feeling of knowing I'd made the biggest mistake of my life. Thank God I have Bre; she's been my best friend since we were nine years old living in Detroit. I ran into her a few years ago after she retired from modeling and moved to Atlanta to be closer to her parents, and we've been inseparable ever since.

Carlos is a sweetheart and a nice guy. He's the youth minister at New Vision International Cathedral. We met during a back-to-school drive where we passed out school supplies and clothes to the children in the community. I'm not attracted to him, but he is handy around the house and can fix things. He has a wife, but that means nothing to me. I don't want him like that. I just need help around the house, since I married a jailbird who is institutionalized. Quiet as it's kept; I'd rather have his wife. She is fine with her saved, sanctified, and filled with the Holy Ghost self. If she lay her religion down, I'd put her in the game.

MICHAEL

ALEXIS PLANE WAS DUE TO arrive at LAX at 5:30 pm. I was beyond excited; I could hardly contain myself. I must have checked the clock on the computer and looked at my watch a hundred times that day. It seemed as if time stood still. My assistant Marla kept coming into my office, disrupting my fantasy. As the Chief Financial Officer, I manually sign every check and purchase order. With all the technological advances it is a shame we don't use electronic signatures. I guess the owner is a little untrusting, but hey, it's his money and he wants to know where every cent goes and who authorized it. I guess I'd be the same way if I had a multi-million dollar company.

I should have left work sooner because the traffic on the 110 was a parking lot as usual. If I am able to drive at least twenty miles per hour in LA traffic, then I'm happy. I hate being late. I don't want my baby to have to stand outside and wait. I learned from some of our phone conversations that Alexis can be a bit moody and I don't want things to get off to a bad start, so I called her to test the pulse of her mood.

"Hi, most beautiful woman!"

"Hi, honey."

"Baby, I'm so sorry; I didn't leave the office on time and now I'm stuck in traffic. My GPS says I should arrive in twenty minutes."

"That's fine, babe, I know LA traffic is the devil. I'll see when you get here."

I'm glad she sounded upbeat and calm. She can go from hot to cold in less than sixty seconds. By the time I pulled up to LAX in my black Mercedes Benz S550 it was six thirty. She was doing something with her phone and didn't even notice me. My baby looked adorable in her black mid-thigh-length shorts and black wedges. She had on a short sleeve black silver rhinestone Michael Kors t-shirt that hugged her body. *Oh Lord, I can't wait to get her in my bed. Dinner might have to wait.* She cut her hair since the cruise and the new style accentuated her facial features well and she looked more beautiful than I last remembered. I love her dimples. All the pictures she sent don't do her justice.

I had to call her cell phone to get her attention. As she walked toward me, I could feel my dick getting hard. *I can't wait to fuck her*. She gave me the biggest smile. I hugged her so hard I was afraid I was going to break her tiny size-four frame. We kissed quickly before I loaded her bags into the car. We couldn't spend too much time in front of the airport loading and unloading zone because the police will start blowing the horn for you to keep moving. I whispered, "Let's get out of here so I can get a real kiss."

"Ok," she blushed.

I loved having my woman sitting next to me. The pictures and videos are great, but they are no substitute for the real thing. Besides, I'm starting to get a little jealous of that pink dildo and I absolutely don't want her to get tired of it and start practicing with someone else. It is approximately 2,420 miles from my front door to hers. I can't just pop up. Leaving LAX the traffic was bumper to bumper. I reached over and held her hand and asked, "So, baby, how was your flight?"

"It was okay. The flight attendant spilled tomato juice on my jacket and the bitch didn't even say sorry or anything."

"Awww, baby, don't worry about that. We can get it cleaned."

"I know; I just think it was rude. You can't cuss them out anymore because they will arrest you for making terroristic threats."

"Oh Lord, what am I going to do with my baby?"

"Pull over and give me a real kiss."

"I can do that," I said as I pulled into the Shell gas station parking lot on Century Blvd.

I leaned in for a kiss. I smelled the perfume I bought her, Euphoria by Calvin Klein. I kissed her with such passion as our tongues intertwined; I felt her hand slowly move up my thigh to my dick. At this moment I loved this woman to death and couldn't wait for her to become Mrs. Olfonse. She was so passionate and beautiful inside and out. I loved the cards she sent the good morning and goodnight text. I loved and appreciated her thoughtfulness. I could hear the fear in her voice as she talked about loving and trusting men again. I know she's been hurt. She won't talk about her past relationships. That doesn't bother me. The past is the past. I look forward to a lifetime with her. When we arrived at my apartment we embraced and kissed each. I wanted to fuck her right in the middle of the living room. When I unbuttoned her shorts and pulled them and her panties down she stopped me.

"Baby, what's wrong?" I asked.

"I have to take a shower, honey, I'm so sweaty. I don't feel fresh."

"I like your sweat." She pushed me away and asked, "What time is our dinner reservation?"

Pulling her close to me, I said, "9:00 pm, so we have plenty of time."

"You're going to start something you can't finish. You know you don't do quickies."

"I will tonight, and then we can go to dinner and come home for dessert." She would not give in. "Okay, go take your shower. I'll be sitting here trying to get my dick to go down."

Teasingly she said, "Awww, I love you...let me kiss him to see if that will make him feel better."

She unzipped my pants and wrapped her tiny soft French manicured hands around my magic stick and kissed it gently. Suddenly she stopped and sauntered away; while looking back she said, "Let me take a shower."

"Oh Lord, woman, you are such a tease."

ALEXIS

MY VISIT TO LA STARTED out great. Michael picked me up from LAX late because he got caught in traffic on the 101. I was tired when I landed; however, when I felt Michael's embrace I received a boost of energy. I was long overdue for a visit and some maintenance. Gazing at his 6'4" frame draped in black slacks with a purple Van Heusen dress shirt and black paisley tie, my va-jay-jay became moist. I loved his melodic Bajan accent; it was soft and sensuous.

We went to his apartment on Burton Way in downtown LA so I could shower before dinner. Of course, I had to give him something to look forward to after dinner. We were hungry and not just for food. I needed to shower after that long flight. When I stepped out of the shower he greeted me with a large beige towel that felt good on my skin. He carried me to the bedroom and laid me on my stomach. Slowly he dried my body with the towel and his touch felt electric. I took a deep breath and exhaled as he carefully caressed my body with coconut oil.

While gazing into my eyes, slowly he kissed my lips and then he stuck his tongue in my mouth and the kisses became intense. I could taste the peppermint in his mouth. My heart was pounding like a drummer at a college football halftime show. I watched him undress and meticulously lay his clothes on the chair. Each time he took off an article of clothing I became more excited, impatient and my breathing became shallower. It had been six months since we made love on the cruise. I had toys, but they didn't hold a candle to my Barbadian lover. Oh, how I loved this man. We spent many hours on the phone discussing everything: our hopes, fears, dreams, and plans for the future. We decided that we would get married within three years. I could be submissive to him. I wasn't afraid to let him lead. I trusted him. I felt in my core that everything would be all right.

He was such a hard worker. He worked as a CFO for a large corporation in LA and owned a small bed and breakfast in Calabasas, CA. He would jokingly say, "Me got tree jobs, me have four in da morning." He was always going from one job to the next, it seemed. His ultimate goal was to work for himself. He always said, "I'm working hard and stressing now, so that when you become my wife you don't have to work." I believed him. I shouldn't have.

* * *

My heart pounded and I felt sick in the pit of my stomach. My mind raced as I tried to hold my composure. I shifted from left to right on the bar stool as I sifted through my tan Dooney and Bourke satchel purse. Michael smiled as he walked towards me and kissed me softly on the lips. My body tensed because I didn't know if I should confront him about my findings or just shrug it off. After all, we hadn't been in a relationship that long and haven't seen each other since we met on the cruise.

I believed him when he said he was not in a relationship and he hadn't been on a date in a while. I tried hard to let it go, but it bothered me. I was unable to focus; my hands were shaking. I needed to know for my own peace of mind. I wasn't sure if I would even believe him. After what happened with Matthew it was hard to trust men. I was prepared to walk away from this relationship before I got my heart broken again. Michael could sense something was wrong. After he kissed me he stepped back and looked at me. I looked down - I didn't want him to see my eyes. My eyes showed everything. I looked up and softly I said, "Are you seeing someone else?"

"No," he replied.

"Ok," I said nonchalantly

He looked at me and said, "Why did you ask me that, baby?"

I tried to play it off and said, "No reason...just wanted to know."

He could tell I was not forthcoming because he said, "Baby, what's wrong? Why do you ask?"

I took a deep breath and said, "Why do you have women's cologne, maxi pads, and Bath & Body Works in your cabinet?"

"Why did you go in my cabinet?"

"Because I wanted to...I saw the bath gloves in the show and figured they belonged to a woman."

Pulling me close he said, "Baby, don't do this to yourself...to us. I am not seeing anyone. Those things belong to my cousin Karen; she cleans for me and she stays here when I go out of town for long periods." I wasn't sure if I believed his explanation but I didn't want to discuss it further, so I said, "Ok."

He continued to explain as we walked to his car. My right eye started twitching. I was getting agitated, so I said, "Oh my God, just let it go, Michael. You've explained already. I've moved on; this conversation is over."

"Are you a jealous woman?" he asked while unlocking the car doors.

"No," I snapped. "I am a good woman and I have a lot to add to a relationship."

"Like what?"

"Love...I love hard, I'm faithful, I support my man and I will do anything for my man, except for going to jail."

"I wouldn't ask you to do anything to go to jail because I'm not going to jail."

"I will spoil my man and I will always have his back."

"I believe that, Alexis, you have a beautiful heart. Trust me, baby, I'm not seeing anyone." A part of me wanted to believe him, but the damaged part of me wanted to cry. I was silent as I stared out the window. The LA traffic was horrible. While waiting to merge onto the freeway he took my hand and said, "Look at me. I am not seeing anyone."

"Michael, please let it go."

"I told you on the phone I was falling in love with you." I ignored him as the sounds of Teddy Pendergrass filled the car. Teddy sang "Nine times out of ten I'm falling in love with you, starting to need you more..." He restarted the track and turned the volume up. My heart melted. He told me numerous times during our late-night conversations that he was falling in love with me and that he was going to marry me. I had heard those words before from Matthew.

When we pulled the car into the parking lot of Roscoe's on Manchester Blvd he kissed me and said, "Are we good?" I could tell from his tone that he didn't want to lose me. "Yeah," I said and we kissed again.

ALEXIS

It's been a week since I've returned from LA and my heart is filled with pain. I thought Michael was the one. You can't share that kind of energy and have that type of connection with someone and it end up being a lie. He was fun, kind, gentle, and his positive energy was contagious. I felt safe with him. I didn't have to be so strong because he was a take-charge kind of guy. He is exactly what a headstrong, independent woman like me needed. He softened me.

As I sat in silence the hum of the ceiling fan and the swishing of the washer calmed me. It was a rainy Sunday morning. My heart was aching. I longed to go outside so the water could hide my tears and hopefully wash away the pain. A part of me wanted it to stop raining so I could go walk Stone Mountain and the other part hoped it never stopped. I sat alone my empty apartment in complete silence disconnected from the world. My cell phone, iPad, and television were off.

I thought I could handle being in a long-distance relationship. I've been in one before and it worked out fine. Long-distance relationships can work, but you have to be honest with your partner. My motto before was, "I don't care about the other girls, just be good to me." Hell, you can't stop a man from cheating even if you're in the same city. The only thing I asked was don't bring me any disease, and when I am in town you better make me feel like I'm the only one. So I was not going to disturb my peace of mind by worry about what he was doing?

At this point in my life I'm tired of sharing a man. Why can't men just tell the damn truth? I guess that why I'm sitting here nursing a broken heart and listening to old school music. I have Miliara's "Go Outside in the Rain" on repeat because I trusted a lying cheating man.

AUTUMN

I WAS WATCHING A SPECIAL on CNN on veterans who suffer from PTSD and the statistics are alarming: 8,000 veterans kill themselves each year. The VA hospital cure for everything seems to be Ambien, Zoloft, Celexa, Prozac, Xanax or some other antidepressant. Its crazy when a soldier returns from deployment all the red tape, paperwork, and long-ass wait time they have to go through to see a health care provider. I hated taking Celexa - I felt numb, like I was a zombie I didn't need antidepressants or sleeping pills before I was deployed and now I do. My eyes looked dull as if I was soulless. The upside to being on medication is that it keeps you from going off on people. I stopped taking my medication when a soldier in my platoon died from mixing antidepressants with sleeping pills and alcohol. I would rather be awake and sleepy than dead and sleeping.

There are all kinds of specials about male soldiers who suffer from PTSD, and hardly anything about female soldiers. A lot of us suffer in silence. Most of us smile and pretend to be strong, pretend to be okay, when inside we are dying. I'm not taking anything away from the males' struggle, but if they have kids they can walk away. Not us. There are days when I want to die. I can't because my fourteen-year-old daughter Morgan needs me even if she thinks she don't. She is probably the only reason I fight hard to live every day. Her deadbeat-ass daddy, Kevin, ain't shit with his part-time parenting. He's salty that he got kicked out of the Army for adultery. His dumb ass wasn't even married when we met and I got pregnant. He married Brenda stanking ass when I was five months pregnant. He thought she could help him with his career because she was a First Sergeant and I was just a Specialist.

When he got married I was crushed, but I still slept with him. I was carrying his baby - hell, I had a right to. I didn't run and tell her I had a baby by her husband; that was his job. Morgan is the spitting image of his raggedy ass. She has his light brown eyes, straight narrow nose, and thick curly black hair. He had the nerve to say he had a vasectomy and since we always used condoms the baby wasn't his. I cussed his ass out from the top to the bottom. The paternity test proved that he was the father. I might be a lot of things; however, whore is not one of them.

I remember the night I got pregnant. We hadn't had sex for three weeks. We decided to stop seeing each other - that lasted about two weeks. As luck would have it the condom broke. He could have pulled out but he kept stroking, so it is what it is. I should have made him stop, especially since I wasn't the only woman he was sleeping with. He was kicking it with Brenda's big ass and some tramp from New Orleans. I didn't know it at the time but that tramp was pregnant too; our babies were born one month apart. After Kevin married that cow he had the nerve to say, "I'll cheat, but I'm not leaving my wife." The only reason I kept letting him come back is because he was great in bed and MSG Temple, my new boo, had relocated to Hawaii. Kevin and I had good times when we were together. Although he was cocky and a little arrogant at times, I did love him. After the CNN special on veterans went off, I texted Lexi.

<u>What are you doing?</u>

<u>Watching TV</u>

<u>Let me guess...Empire</u>

<u>Yes</u>

<u>I'm getting ready to call you, so answer the phone.</u>

<u>K</u>

"Hello?" Lexi answered.

"Girl, are you sitting down?"

"Why?"

"I almost went to jail Saturday."

"Jail! For what, Dani?!"

"Don't call me Dani. I go by Autumn."

"Whatever, trick...what happened? Why are you just now calling? It's Wednesday."

"I know what day it is. Just listen. I hit Kevin's ass in the head with a weed whacker."

"Do you mean weed eater?"

"Whacker/eater, same thing."

"Y'all and that ghetto drama. What happened?"

"Girl, this petty bastard came over with some of his buddies from their little Corvette club. They stopped by the house...anyway, Morgan wasn't home. She was at Chuck E. Cheese with Bre and KJ. So we're outside talking and Mr. Reed from next door came over to look at the cars. Everyone's just standing around chopping it up. I got a phone call so I went in the house to talk. A few minutes later here comes Kevin's old ass. I don't know how he got that fancy car, but he's always late on his child support."

"Girl, you are a fool. Go on with the story."

"He had the nerve to say 'tell that nigga your baby daddy is here so you can't talk.'"

"No, he didn't. He needs to have several seats."

"Right! His goofy ass showed out. Started talking all loud, talking 'bout 'when is my daughter coming so I can see her and get the hell away from here?'"

"Oh, so now he wants to see his daughter."

"That's not the bad part. Then he said, 'Bitches ain't shit!' I was like, who you calling a bitch!"

"No, he didn't call you a bitch! That trifling sorry-ass excuse for a man."

"He got all up in my face and started pointing his finger talking about YOU! 'How you going to disrespect me and be on the phone with some nigga?' I was like, motherfucker, you ain't my man, you got a wife. You need to worry about her.' Then he started blaming me for getting put out of the military.

"He needs to let that go and move on. How long has it been since he got put out? I can't stand him. He needs to act like he's over fifty and take responsibility for his own actions."

"That's what I told him. I walked back outside and he called me a bitch again. I snapped! That's when I picked up the weed whacker and started swinging it like a golf club. When he backed away from me he fell. I guess his ego and his ass was bruised because when he got up he slapped me so hard and fast in my face my ears were ringing. He knows I can't hardly hear. Then he had the nerve to walk away like it was over. I took that weed whacker."

"Weed eater."

"Whatever. I hit his ass in the back of the head." I thought the call had dropped because there was dead silence. "Hello?" I said. "Are you still there?" I asked.

"Yes, I'm here."

"Why you so quiet?"

"I'm trying to keep from laughing," Alexis busted out laughing.

"It's not funny, Lexi; I was so mad I saw red. His friend Brandon asked me if it was okay to leave Kevin's car at my house while they took him to Grady Hospital."

"Did the police come?"

"Yep, they showed up and asked him if he wanted to press charges. They told me I could press charges too since he hit me first. So he said no."

"I'm surprised they didn't take both of y'all to jail. I swear minorities always keeping up shit."

"Whatever! Kevin knows that I'm crazy and I didn't just get crazy today."

"Did you tell your parents?"

"No, Mom would have had a fit. You know she's so extra and dramatic."

"True. Girl, let me get off this phone. I need to get ready for work."

"Lexi."

"What?"

"Do you want to go to a comedy show with me?"

"When? Where? What time?"

"Cosmopolitan Restaurant. The show starts at 8:00 pm. I want to introduce you to someone. He is really nice and fine. I think you would like him."

"Yes, I will go. Stop trying to be a matchmaker. I just want to laugh and enjoy the show. I'm done dating for a while. Besides, if he is so fine why are you not keeping him for yourself?"

"Honey, he is not my type. That's why I put him in the friend zone."

"Bye, crazy, love you!"

"Bye, love you, too." I love talking to my big sis. I can't wait to introduce her to Xavier. I hope they make a love connection. She's going to be shocked when she finds out who he is.

AUBREY

THIS WAS MY SECOND VISIT to see Dr. Johnson. He came highly recommended. He had a striking resemblance to my father. He's fair-skinned, about 6'1", and he has dreads with blond tips. He has a broad nose and thin lips. He could really pass for my father's brother. When I walked into his office I sat in the same chair as before, the oversized brown leather chair closest to the window. I am not sure why because the only view is of Westwood College.

What made me decide to see a mental health professional again was his therapy approach was different from the others. He used something called a narrative therapy approach, which separates the person from the problem. Dr. J gives a person the chance to tell or retell their story, which he calls testify. Narrative therapy seeks to empower and recognizes that people have the competencies, skills, and expertise that can help them change their lives. Rather than changing the person narrative therapy goal is to change the effects on the problem. This is the type of therapy I needed my past is running rampant in my present.

"Hello, Aubrey, how are you today?" Dr. J asked.

"I'm here."

"What does that mean?"

"Nothing, really, it's just hard to deal with the traffic on 85S and it always put me in a bad mood."

"Bad mood? Why does the traffic put you in a bad mood?"

"Like my sister Lexi always says, 'It makes my spirit heavy.'"

"I remember you mentioning your sisters our last visit. Did you tell them that you are seeing a mental health professional?"

"No, I haven't told anyone."

"Do you plan on telling your family?"

"I doubt it."

"Why? Your family could be a good source of support."

"I'll deal with this by myself. My family doesn't understand me."

"Alright then, let's change the subject. Are you still having those dreams?"

"Yes."

"Would you like to talk about them?"

"Not really."

"Okay, no pressure. You can talk about them when you are ready."

I stared at the Westwood sign so hard my eyes crossed. I could hear Dr. J, but his voice sounded like Charlie Brown's teacher.

"Have you been doing the EFT Tapping Technique?"

"No, I haven't had time."

"We make time for what's important to us...tell me, Aubrey, why are you here? I'm sure you could find other ways to spend your money and your time."

I ignored his question and statement and gazed at the bird on the bookcase with his head turned to the back. "What is that?" I asked. *I can do whatever I want with my money.*

"It's Sankofa, which is a symbol of the importance of learning from the past. It means 'return and get,'" he replied. He really is handsome, but looks too much like my daddy. I guess I will not cross that line; otherwise, he could get it.

"Oh" I said.

"Last week you talked briefly about your brother's death and how you feel responsible." Here he goes with this again. I should not have mentioned Aaron. "You mentioned he died in a fire."

"Yes, our house caught fire when we lived in Detroit. Everything happened so fast. I heard Aaron crying for help but we couldn't get to him...it was too much smoke. He was trapped in his bedroom." I paused and looked out the window and then said, "I am having dreams about him. I can hear him calling my name...he was my twin."

"What are you doing in the dream?"

"I am trying to save him from the fire." Then in a voice I barely recognize as my own and for the first time ever, I whispered, "It was my fault. I started the fire because I was smoking."

ALEXIS

I LOVE MY SISTERS BUT I wish they would stop trying to fix me up. I haven't gotten settled into my Midtown apartment. I rented a two-bedroom, I disliked the floor plan for the one-bedroom your guest have to walk through your bedroom to get to the bathroom. I don't want people walking through my bedroom. Also, I don't want everyone sitting their asses on my toilet. The building has: a swimming pool with a waterfall, cabana lounges, and private grilling areas. The view from my tenth-floor apartment is breathtaking. There is a fitness center in the building. Everything I need is right at my fingertips. Sometimes I go to the Skyline viewing room and sip on my favorite cocktail, Coconut Ciroc and pineapple juice.

After the drama with Matthew and then with Michael I needed to heal before I start dating again. I am tired of sleeping by myself. I want unconditional love, someone who is going to be true, and who is afraid of losing me. I can't put my heart out there again. Not yet.

AUTUMN

I WAS HAPPY ALEXIS AGREED to ride with me tonight. As usual we arrived before Bre and Vanessa. Bre is always late, so her tardiness is nothing new. The monthly jazz and jokes shows are nice. The atmosphere is intimate and can be downright romantic with the right man. They always have a funny line-up of comedians and the musical guests are awesome.

The hostess seated us at the table right in front of the stage. "Why do we have to be so close to the stage?" Alexis asked. I can't understand how a person who is the host of her own radio show hates attention. "Girl, these are great seats. Relax and order some wine and some food." These are perfect. I can see the door. Xavier should be here soon; he is the headliner and he likes to arrive early so he can watch the crowd. I looked up and saw Aubrey and Vanessa standing at the entrance. "Bre, we're over here," I yelled.

"Really, Dani? So you just are going to holler out in this nice establishment?"

"Hush, Lexi, and stop calling Dani. I go by Autumn now. I had to get their attention. Shit, I'm surprised they made it before the show started."

"Hi, Divas!" Bre said.

"Hi, ladies," Vanessa said.

"I'm so glad to get out of the house...I need a break," Bre said while plopping down in her seat.

"Break? Your ass don't do nothing!" I said.

I don't know why she always complains. This heffa has a husband and she works from home, but she needs a break. She can miss me with that.

She should try raising a teenager alone and working at a dead-end job where you can't even make ends meet. This heffa's ends are overlapping. Her spoiled ass needs to take a walk in my shoes. She better be glad that I wanted to have a good time; otherwise, I would have read her like a book.

"So where is the mystery man?" Lexi asked.

"Stop being so impatient, Lexi; he will be here. Don't worry," I reassured her.

When the waitress came I ordered a glass of Moscato. "I hope he's fine and established." I gave Bre the side eye after that comment. All she thinks about is money and status. I'm surprised she even got a husband. "Why are you worried about how established he is? He's here to meet Lexi, not you. You got a man." I patted Lexi's arm and said, "Don't worry, Lexi, he's a keeper."

"I'm not concerned with looks and I don't need him to pay my bills. As long as he don't need me to help pay his bills it's all good. If I don't ask him to pay Verizon he don't need to ask me to pay Metro PCS." I shook my head; Lexi's ass can be so funny.

"I just hope he's working with something. How tall is he?" Lexi asked.

"Girl, height doesn't matter."

"It does to me. A man's got to be over six feet tall to ride this ride," Lexi laughed.

"I know some tall brothers with big hands and feet who came up short," I said.

We all busted out laughing. I loved hanging out with my sisters. We talk about any and everything. Bre always gets quiet as a church mouse when we talk about sex. I guess being married to a preacher; it would be a sin to talk about having sex outside of marriage.

"Don't say anything about the big feet and hands myth. I dated this guy who was 6'6" and his penis was so small I didn't know whether to tell him to put his drawers back on or hand him a Huggie. It's a shame a grown-ass man walking around with a lil' baby wee wee," Lexi added.

The coconut rum, pineapple and cranberry juice Lexi was drinking must have kicked in because she will say anything, especially when she's had a cocktail.

"Lexi, I can't take you serious," I laughed. I looked towards the door and Xavier was walking in carrying a black backpack. "There's Xavier. Xa, over here!" I yelled and waved to get his attention. Lexi cut her eyes at me and shook her head.

"Hello, beautiful ladies," he greeted us.

"Hey," we said in unison.

"Xavier, these are my big sisters, Lexi and Bre. And this is Vanessa, our adopted sister."

"It is nice to meet you, ladies. I've heard so much about you," Xavier said while looking at Alexis.

"All good, I hope," Lexi said.

"Of course, I wouldn't say anything bad about my two beautiful sisters," I interjected.

"Sure, you wouldn't," Aubrey said while raising her eyebrows.

"Well, ladies, let me go see where I can set up my merchandise and make sure the promoter has my money. I will talk to you later. Enjoy the show."

"He is fine! You know I had a crush on him since the first time I saw him perform."

"Well, so it's safe to say that he can get it."

"Girl, yes!"

"Is that all you two talk about every time we get together?"

"Listen, Mrs. First Lady, don't hate on me and Lexi because we don't act like prudes." I understand that Bre is the First Lady of New Vision International Cathedral, one of Atlanta's mega-churches, but she is so uuhhh.

"Well, I could talk about the injustice in this world. Cops killing black men like its deer season. And don't get me started on black-on-black crime.

Sixty-five people killed in Chicago in one weekend. Black folks don't get in an uproar about black-on-black crime, but go ham when a white person does the same thing they are doing," I ranted.

"Please, we are not the only race who kills one another. There is a whole network dedicated to white folks killing; it's called Investigation Discovery. Anyway, don't get Autumn X started. Let's have a peaceful evening." It's just like Lexi to be the peace maker.

"Okay, let's finish talking about sex." I said while glancing at Bre. She rolled her eyes.

"I was thinking about going to one of my co-workers passion parties. I think we should all go. I attended one and it was fun! We ate and drank while looking at all the adult toys."

"That sounds like fun, I'm in." I knew Alexis' freaky ass would be on board.

"Are you going, Bre Bear?"

"I hate when you call me that, Alexis!"

"Whatever, heffa, are you going?" Alexis said. I turned to Vanessa and said, "Vanessa, would you like to come?"

"Nessa, don't let them drag you into that mess," Bre interrupted. Ignoring her Vanessa replied, "Sure, I think it would be fun."

"I think it would be fun, too...come on, Bre, don't be a party pooper. We can have a girls' night out," Alexis said.

"So it's settled. We are going," I said.

The host stepped on stage and said, "Welcome to Jazz and Jokes." I looked at the time on my cell phone; it was eight forty-five. *We are always on colored people time.*

AUBREY

THE COSMOPOLITAN RESTAURANT IN MARIETTA was nice; the food was good, the music was excellent, and the comedians were funny. However, my sisters got on my last nerves with all their talk about sex. They think they got the "freak between the sheets" game on lock. I could teach them a thing or two about pleasing someone in the bedroom and show them how to take their freak meter up to ten. That is why I have a husband and a girlfriend.

They don't know me. They think because Kai is a Bishop that I am some kind of puritan. I have no inhibitions when it comes to sex; however, my husband does so I have to get my desires fulfilled in other ways. I keep telling him that the marriage bed is undefiled and that's Biblical, but like most Christians he picks and choose the part of the Bible he wants to follow. He used to try different things in the bedroom before God called him to preach and now he is so holier-than-thou he's boring.

I used to love spending time with Vanessa. She wanted to go to a hotel after the show but I had to get home. She is starting to get too needy and all the crazy talk about coming out the closet. I have the best of both worlds. She is going to make me end this arrangement if she don't get out of her feelings. I hire and fire; I just got rid of Eric's lying ass. After a year it was time for him to go. He didn't mind selling his ass for money and that dumb bitch that he is married to is a whore. They pimp each other. The first time I saw her at church I could look in her eyes and tell she was slow; she even walks and talks slow. Who in their right mind would knowingly put up with their spouse cheating year after year? When do you say enough is enough? As much dirt as I do and all the skeletons in my closet I don't think I would put up with Kai cheating.

I'm not attached to nor do I have real feelings for any of the flings I've had, except for Vanessa. If things were different I could be with her and only her. I'm afraid of what my family would say. Lord knows, I can only imagine what my mom would say. She would probably never talk to me again in life. Although being gay is widely accepted in Atlanta I still feel like I have to hide that part of my life. I guess Vanessa is right; I am in the closet. I want to be my true authentic self. All my life I have been a people-pleaser so I have lived my life with so many secrets. My saving grace is KJ and my design firm, and if I can get my show idea picked up for HGTV it will take my design firm and career to the next level. I can live with the other unsatisfying parts of my life.

Vanessa's ringtone startled me. I didn't feel like talking to her; I have too much on my plate. I took a deep breath and said, "What's up, Nessa?"

"What are you doing?" I hate when she asks me that; for some reason it makes my blood boil. I responded, "Working on my pitch for my show idea and then later KJ has a playdate."

"Oh, I didn't want anything. I was calling to see if you wanted to go shopping." Shopping was our code word for hooking up. As bad as I needed to relieve some stress I had work to do. "Sorry, hun, I will have to take a rain check."

"Lately all I've been getting is a rain check. When can I cash out?"

"Nessa, you know getting my own television show is important to me so I have a lot of work to do."

"I understand. I just miss you."

"I miss you, too; that is why I am glad we got a chance to hang out at the comedy show."

"Don't be coy, Bre, you know what I'm talking about." I didn't want to lose my temper, so silently I counted to ten and then responded, "Listen, we are not going to do this today."

"Do what?" Her dumb act pissed me off. "You know...this back and forth bullshit. I told you that I am busy. I have too much going on so you will have to be patient or we can end this." I didn't give her a chance to respond; I just hung up the phone.

VANESSA

Bre is starting to get on my nerves. I'm tired of her excuses. I would give up this charade of liking men and be with her exclusively if she would stop lying to herself and living her life for everyone else. I don't ask for much; I never make demands. I got feelings and needs. Men don't do it for me.

Her excuse today was she's working on her show idea for HGTV and Kai Jr. has a playdate. What the hell?! She knows I would never impose on her family time and she takes advantage of it. She has one more time to hang up the phone on me and I'm done. I'm tired of being disappointed and getting my feelings hurt. The next time I won't be the only one with hurt feelings.

ALEXIS

I COULD KILL AUTUMN! SHE didn't tell me Xavier was comedian Xavier Arnold. I haven't seen him in years; I always wondered if he was still doing comedy. He's a well-spoken and well-dressed brother. It's refreshing to meet a grown man who knows how to carry a decent conversation. The brother was wearing the hell out of the navy blue suit with a pink and blue paisley pocket square. He is a little shorter than I like - he appeared to be about 5'11" and I like my men to be over six feet. I'll make exceptions for this pecan-colored, bald fade, muscular-built specimen of a man. I loved the way he greeted us. We were used to being called beautiful, but the smooth melodic rhythm of his voice...there was something about his voice, so sexy and smooth and comforting. His deer eyes were sexy. Xavier piqued my interest. We exchanged numbers after the show and he promised to call me the next day.

He called the next evening. I was impressed that he called and did not text. I hate when you give a person your number and they only communicate through text messages. I even had a sorry-ass man ask me for a date via text message. Xavier and I talked for hours and before we ended the conversation he asked me out on a date. We agreed that he would pick me up at 8:00 pm and we would go to dinner and a movie.

I could tell when we first met at Cosmopolitan Restaurant, we had chemistry. When he sat down next to me the sexual attraction was strong and his closeness to me aroused all my senses. My heart was beating so fast I knew that my body temperature had increased. It felt as if I was having hot flashes. He definitely can get it anytime anywhere. I hope he is not like a lot of men who block their blessing by talking too much. I try to tell brothers on my radio show that women know within minutes of meeting a guy if she'll have sex with them, but they mess it up by saying stupid shit. My advice to men is if you've been chosen get some pie, then get somewhere, sit down, and pray that the Lord will put an electric fence around your mouth that will shock you if you say the wrong things.

I don't have a ninety-day rule; I am a grown woman and if I want to get some it ain't nobody's business. Besides, if he is not good in bed, then I don't want to waste three months before I find out he sucks. I hoped this was a true soul connection and not lust. I would soon find out.

AUTUMN

SPEAKING IS FREE. I'M AMAZED at the lengths people will go through to keep from speaking, this idiot almost walked into the wall because he was looking down to keep from making eye contact. I'll be so happy when I can leave Sodom and Gomorrah. This is undeniably Peyton Place. At least it's Friday. I swear the wrong kind of job will have you rushing towards Friday and I am not sure how many Fridays I have left. I entered my office like a robot. First I turned on the radio, then my electric heater, and then my computer. When John Legend started singing, I changed the radio station from Steve Harvey to Tom Joyner. How many times are they going to play his whining-ass song? Steve gives some good advice, but I don't think every woman's mission in life is to get a wedding ring, dress, and some damn cake. Marriage is work and if you are not willing to put in the work don't mess with it. A bad relationship can make you bitter or better and this world has enough bitter, hateful, and damaged people.

Let Lexi tell it: we attract what we are and if we fix ourselves and love ourselves we will attract the right people. She gets on my nerve with that Super Soul bullshit. Some people are just fucked up and needs to be slapped in the face with a brick. Social media is the devil's spawn and will ruin a relationship. There are so many broken attention-seeking people who put all their business on Facebook. Then you have those who get in their feelings when you don't like their status. So many people who want you to follow them on Twitter, Instagram, and whatever else.

I already felt some kind of way when I arrived at work. Just when I thought things couldn't get any worse, David walked in. How many women does he think he can pull in the same organization?

He got life messed up if he thinks I'm going to give him the time of day. I swear married men with single men feelings get on my last nerve. They act single and like they are a hot commodity in Atlanta because women outnumber the men. Men these days really think a woman is so desperate to have a man they will pay them. I don't make enough money to take care of a grown rusty-ass man. I have a child to feed and clothe. You can't even get these sorry men to cut the grass. I'm tired of married men, I'm tired of this job, I'm tired of Kevin's sorry ass, and I'm tired of not sleeping at night. I'm tired of being sick and tired.

Last night my girl Wendy invited me to Laugh Your Class Off Comedy show. This little runt of a man, whose pants and shirt were so little he probably bought them from Babies 'R' Us, asked me to hook him up with Wendy, but then killed any chance he might have had by saying, "I want to get with your friend, but I ain't shit." I gave him a blank stare and then said, "she ain't shit either, so y'all be ain't shit together."

It's a shame some men pride themselves on not being shit. I can appreciate the brother's honesty. More men should be like him, or at least come with a stamp or something on their forehead. I'm done dating 'ain't shit' brothers," and even though my friends try to convince me to date outside my race, I can't. I love my brothers. I believe that my King is out there; I just need a flashlight and a flare to find him.

So for now I'm just going to work on a better me, so I can attract what I am. In the meantime, I will keep pushing the lawnmower and fixing stuff on my own. I am so glad my daddy taught us how to do small do-it-yourself projects so we could be independent. I'm beginning to think that independence is overrated I need some help!

I'm really thinking about trying stand-up comedy. I think I got jokes. Most of the people in the ATL think they got jokes and don't. Bless their hearts for trying. The host of *Laugh Your Class Off* gave me his business card. I might call and see if I can get onstage at their next show. *Oh God, I need a new occupation. Who in the world is calling my cell phone at eight o'clock in the morning? I hope it is not my mother calling being nosy or with drama.* I don't allow people to call me early in the morning with their drama. If they couldn't work out their drama last night when they went to bed, then there is nothing I can do this early in the morning. I have enough of my own with Morgan's daddy. I started not to answer, since I didn't recognize the number. "Hello?" I said. The caller hung up.

ALEXIS

Xavier picked me up at 7:15 pm. He looked gorgeous in his tan with light-blue-striped suit. He wore a light blue shirt, a Carolina blue and brown paisley tie, and brown Stacy Adams. When he hugged me I could smell his *Bond No 9 Scent of Peace for Him*. I haven't seen him in three weeks because he's been on tour. I didn't realize how much I missed him. We talked at least twice a day. I could set my watch by his good morning call. I loved when he says, "What's up, lil' mama?" The comedy show was great! My boo was so funny. A man with a sense of humor is sexy to me. Add intelligence, hard worker, and swag and I am hooked.

We arrived back to my Midtown apartment at about 11:30 pm. I led Xavier to my beige leather sofa. Xavier pulled me close and gently kissed my forehead. His soft lips moved slowly to my eyelids, the tip of my nose, and then my lips. My body became relaxed and agile as if I was floating on air. His touch was soft. I could feel the pounding of my heart and my breathing became shallow with anticipation of making love to him. I loved the way he took control. In that moment I became submissive to his touch... his kisses. "Wait!" I said as I slipped from his embrace. When I tried to walk away my knees buckled like a baby calf. "I'll be back," I whispered. I lit candles in the bathroom and turned the shower on. I put on my slow jams playlist on my iPad. I undressed and called Xavier into the bathroom. As I unbuttoned his shirt I let my towel fall to the floor. I planted kisses on his chest as I unzipped his pants. He stepped out of his pants and underwear at the same time. Once he was completely undressed he led me to the shower. As the warm water from the rain forest showerhead rained down on us we hugged and kissed like a lion and lioness in the wild. He pinned my hands against the wall and we made love.

AUBREY

TODAY WAS A GOOD DAY. No, it was better than good; it was great. I finally had a meeting to pitch my show idea to a television network. Although it was not with HGTV I was still excited. During the three-hour meeting I showed my design portfolio and answered a lot of questions. I drove out of the parking lot feeling great, and since I hadn't eaten anything I decided to treat my inner fat girl, so I stopped at Wal-Mart on Howell Mill Rd to buy some Doves chocolate-covered almonds. By the time I got to the cash register, I had Lay's Wavy Ranch potato chips, Magnum double chocolate ice cream bars, and a Tombstone double meat pizza. This was going to be a junk food and Lifetime day.

I was glad Kai and KJ were in Davenport, Iowa visiting his parents for the weekend. For two days I did not have to take care of a single soul. This was a rare moment and I was going to relish it. I didn't mind being on my period because it kept me at home, even though I found a work-around for that. Kai won't come close to me when it's that time of month, but thank God for having an ace in the hole. What he won't do another man or woman will. I love soft cups; they are much better than tampons or pads and they allow you to still have sex. I was going to invite Vanessa over since we hadn't spent any quality time together, but decided against it. I flipped back and forth between Lifetime Movie Network and Investigation Discovery and when I got tired of watching white people killing their spouses for money, I switched to HGTV.

I finally mustard the energy to get off the couch and suddenly I felt sad, like I wanted to die. I tried to walk it off along with the empty calories from the chips, ice cream, and candy, but the feeling would not subside.

I wondered who would find my body if I took my own life. Out of all my family and friends I had no one to call. I briefly thought about calling Dr. J or a suicide hotline. I walked, cried, and prayed for strength for something to lighten my spirit. I walked downstairs to the bar and fixed a glass of Cruzan Coconut Rum with orange-mango juice and a splash of cranberry juice and started cleaning.

ALEXIS

FOREPLAY STARTS IN THE MIND it creates anticipation. Anticipation is what I created twelve days before I flew to Los Angeles to meet Xavier. I sexted him every morning and sent thirty to forty-five-second goodnight videos. I made sure no matter where he was I stayed on his mind. When I arrived at LAX, I went into the small overcrowded bathroom and changed from my Grey Calvin Klein dress and Michael Kors pumps to black lace thigh high stockings, a black micro mini, black and red plaid leather corset, and red open-toe pumps. The temperature in LA was sixty-three degrees, so I didn't look suspicious wearing a trench coach. When I stepped back and opened my white trench coat Xavier was speechless.

My heart felt heavy as we entered the freeway. Xavier is a wonderful person, but he did not hold a candle to Michael in the bedroom. I loved Xavier's sense of humor; however, the energy with him is not the same as it was with Michael. I performed fellatio on Xavier while he was driving - when the car started swerving, I stopped, sat up, and smiled. Ain't nobody got time to be dying while sucking dick.

I saw the exit that led to Michael's house and I had a flashback of when we first met on the cruise. I'll never forget the night we met. My sisters and I were at Ladies Night in the Adriatic Lounge and I noticed this 6'4" chocolate brother looking at me. Finally, he walked over to me and introduced himself. I fell in love with his soft rhythmic accent. We spent a lot of time together on the ship, just talking and getting to know each other. He was divorced after being married for fifteen years. I saw the hurt in his eyes and heard the pain in his voice as he retold the story of being cheated on. "It felt like someone picked my pocket" he said. I bit my bottom lip to keep from laughing. I had never heard that analogy used for cheating. "It seems like you liked being married," I said.

"Yes, I did."

"Would you do it again?"

"Of course, but this would be my last time. People start to think you are a joke if you do it more than three times."

Laughing, I said, "Why do you say that?"

"Because if you can't make a second marriage work, then something might be wrong with you and you should not go down the aisle again."

"I guess you have a point. Sometimes you have to look inside yourself and see what is wrong with you. It is not always the other person," I said.

"I would marry you, you beautiful woman."

I smiled as I laid my head on his shoulder and whispered, "I would marry you, too."

I looked at the bumper to bumper traffic on the 101. Fuck Michael; his feelings were bruised when he got cheated on, yet he turned around and did the same thing to me. "We are here, baby," Xavier said as we pulled up in front of the Marriott. I became present to my surroundings. This is the same hotel where I caught Michael and the waitress from Panda Inn. Suddenly I was no longer excited to be here.

KAI

I WAS SO EXCITED TO be back in the Quad Cities. I wish Aubrey would have come with me and KJ. However, she couldn't leave because she had the meeting to pitch the idea for her TV show. I know how important that is to her. Besides, she probably needs a break from me and KJ and just have some me time. Moms will be watching KJ while I hang out with the boys. When I crossed the I-74 Bridge I felt nostalgic. Every time I come home I have to eat at all my favorite spots, Happy Joe's Pizza, Alfano's Pizza, and Jim's Rib Haven.

Mom was sitting on the front porch when I pulled up to the house. When I walked up the steps she hugged me and took KJ out of my arms and walked in the house. "Why Aubrey didn't come?" she asked.

"I told you, Mom, she had an important meeting that she couldn't miss."

"Mmmphh...she think she's too good to come to Iowa."

I wasn't about to entertain my mom because Shirley knows everything and talking to her is like talking to a door. I attempted to change the subject, so I asked, "Where is James?"

"He's running around here somewhere. I don't hear from him until he needs money."

"You still giving him money?"

"I 'clare for God, every time I think I have some extra money this boy need something. If he ain't short on his rent he need to get that raggedy-ass Jaguar out of the shop; it stay in the shop more than it stay in front of his house."

"How you buy a car and can't afford the upkeep?"

"I don't know. I guess he is trying to keep up with the Joneses. I can't have nothing fooling with him."

My older brother is a mess. He swears he's been called to preach and he's a preacher until he gets mad and then he starts cussing. This clown started a Gofundme account to help with his living expenses because his church doesn't have that many members. He asked me to give him money from my congregation tithes and offering. "You can just give me the money you collect from the overflow room" he said. I didn't entertain him. *Coming home it's always something.* I put our suitcases in my old bedroom and started unpacking. All of a sudden my mom peaked her head in the door and whispered, "Come here...this nigga done been in the shower for twenty-five minutes. Who uses that much water?"

"Who, Mom?"

"Steve!"

"What is he doing here?"

"He lost his job, so I told him they could stay here until he finds something else."

My mom knows she handicaps her sons. Every time I call or come home one of them has moved back in or has borrowed money that they never pay back. I love being home, but these people never change. It is like they don't try to do better. "So, how long has he been here?"

"About six months. He try to cook. I wish he wouldn't because he be messing up my meat and stuff."

"He don't buy groceries?"

"Yes, they like microwave stuff. I don't eat stuff like that and when he does cook he either uses too much salt or too much sugar in his food. My body be so confused; it don't know when to die."

I busted out laughing. Only my mom would say something crazy like that. "Don't let him give you no food with his special sauce." I started laughing again, I remembered how as a teenager he would always put together meals that didn't match. I'm not thinking about Steve and his special sauce my first stop for food is Happy Joe's.

What's up K?

Nothing, I texted back.

I heard you were in the QC. We need to meet. I want to introduce you to someone.

I swear news travels fast. I only told a handful of people that I was coming home, so how in the world did Deidra Williams know I was back in town?

ALEXIS

I LOVE MY JOB BUT I want to change time slots and be on the afternoon drive. My ultimate goal is have my own nationally-syndicated show. In the meantime I'm using this as stepping stone to something bigger. Also, I'm going to start an organization for side chicks. Some women swear they won't be a side chick and if they have been most won't keep it one hundred and admit it. Cheating and being a side chick is a taboo subject. I want my sisters to join me. I haven't pitched the idea yet, but I will Sunday when we meet at Pappadeux for brunch.

I was writing the plan for Side Chicks Unite, LLC when my phone rang, "Hello."

"Hello most beautiful lady."

"Michael?"

"Yes, Alexis...you didn't recognize my number?"

"No I deleted all your contact information."

"Oh Lord. I was thinking about you. I miss you. Do you miss me or think about me?"

"Why are you calling me?" I asked.

"I messed up. Like I said I miss you and have been thinking about you. I will always love you." I didn't respond. I hung up the phone. I can't believe Michael just called and asked if I miss him or if I think about him. Deep down I still loved him, but I refuse to be cheated on. I knew that being in a long-distance relationship would be difficult. However, if he wanted it to be an open relationship he should have said so in the beginning. Men can be so selfish. They want to be the only one to date other people. The first time I caught him in a lie I told him that I could deal with the truth, but not a lie. I do miss him. We didn't have any inhibitions in the bedroom; he tried to outdo Christian Grey in *Fifty Shades of Grey*. I'm sure in his previous life he was in "movies" in LA; that is the code word for porn star. He didn't have a red room, but he did have a bound chair with handcuffs. You really have to trust a man to let him restrict you to a chair and put handcuffs on you, because you are at his mercy.

I blinked to keep the tears from flowing. I refused to cry. I have cried so many tears over so many men and I am so over it. I love him so much that it has affected my relationship with Xavier. I no longer wanted him to touch me because I yearned for Michael's touch. The other day he tried to kiss me and I turned my face so he could only kiss my cheeks. He didn't say anything - he just walked off and got in his car. My cell phone rang again. The number was blocked. I normally don't answer those calls, but I thought Michael might be calling back and blocked his number since I hung up on him.

"Hello," I said.

"Bitch, I know you are messing with my husband!"

"Excuse me? Who in the fuck is this and who is your husband?" I yelled.

"You fucking that many men you don't know who's married and who's not? I guess you think 'cause you on the radio, you can do what you want. Well, leave my man alone!"

"Look, bitch! I don't know your husband so unless you're going to tell me who he is don't call me with this bullshit."

"My husband is Xavier Arnold and I know all about your little affair."

"Xavier?!" I said. I was shocked. How could this be? He said he was divorced. All the trips and all the nights he stayed at my apartment. He has clothes and a toothbrush here. All I could say was, "I'm sorry, I didn't know...what is your name?" I stuttered.

"My name is Sheila Arnold."

"Listen, Sheila, I had no idea Xavier was married. He told me he was divorced."

"Well, he isn't and I would appreciate it if you stop seeing him."

After a short pause I said, "Don't worry, I don't ever want to see his sorry lying ass again." I hung up the phone and dialed his number, but he didn't answer. So I texted him: I received a call from your wife and then I blocked his number.

I can't deal with this—another deceptive man. Why do I keep attracting married men? If they have a wife or a girlfriend then they migrate towards me. I felt a mixture of emotions: I was hurt, pissed, confused. Now more than ever I wanted revenge.

ALEXIS

AUTUMN AND I ORDERED FOOD and drinks while we waited for Aubrey. She is always late for everything. Of course, she had an explanation for her tardiness and then had the audacity to chastise us for scheduling brunch on Sunday. "Sundays are difficult, being the first lady and all," she said. We gave her a blank stare. I turned up my nose, handed her a menu, and said "We've already ordered." She is not that important at that bougie church and most of the women don't like her because they want Kai.

When our food arrived I started the pitch. "One of the reasons I wanted us to meet for brunch is to discuss a business venture that will make us a lot of money," I said. When I mentioned making money Autumn put her fork down and listened intently. I looked at Aubrey her face was stoic. So I continued in a slow steady pace. "I am starting an organization called Side Chicks Unite."

"Called who unite? Aubrey said.

"Wait, hear me out. As you know, mistress, side chick, part-time lover, jump-off or whatever fancy term you want to use has been around since Biblical times."

"You said all that to say what?" Aubrey interrupted.

I rolled my eyes and kept talking. "A man having a woman on the side is international behavior. For instance, I read that China has a system that supports and even encourages cheating. The term for mistress in China is 'ernai,' which means 'second wife.' These woman are supported financially by these men, they live in furnished apartments, drive luxury cars, and receive a monthly living allowance. Critics will say that this is another form of prostitution..."

"Where are you going with this, Alexis?" Autumn interrupted.

"I'm trying to explain. Stop interrupting me. People are going to cheat, so I was thinking we can provide a platform to help them while getting paid, too." For the first time both of my sisters were quiet. "In China when the ladies leave the relationship some are multi-millionaires, they own properties, have businesses, their education is paid for."

"Alexis, this is not China!" Aubrey said.

"I know this is not China, but how many side chicks in America can say that? Most leave the relationship with nothing, maybe a baby, and a broken heart."

Autumn asked, "Are you talking about running a brothel? Is this legal? I can't go to jail...I have Morgan. Plus, the VA will take your disability benefits if you go to jail for longer than six months."

"No, not a brothel. I'm not talking about opening a house where random men run in and out and have sex with the women. I am talking about having an apartment community where the women can stay if they would like and have men take care of them. Listen, men are going to cheat, so why let them cheat for free? Let's make it cost them something besides time."

"I am the first lady of New International! I cannot be a part of this type of mess. It is wrong! It is a sin!"

"Bre, I knew you were going to say that. I was thinking the women could hire your design firm to decorate their apartment and their sponsor will pay for it. Also, I would like to buy an apartment complex, so I might need you to invest a few coins."

"I will not decorate your small village of Sodom and Gomorrah, nor will I invest my 'coins' as you so ghetto fabulously put it. Alexis, I am ashamed of you; you are the oldest and you are supposed to set an example. What has happened to you? Have all those bad relationships made you this bitter and twisted?"

"Hell yeah, I'm bitter. Don't you dare judge me, little Miss High and Mighty first lady. I am grown and unlike you, 'miss I need to please everyone,' I live my life on my own terms and I don't give two fucks what anyone thinks. I got to live and die for Alexis. Now you don't have to be a part of it, nor do you have to decorate; I was just trying to do business with you."

"Do business? I don't want any part of this mess."

"I might not need your money. I was mainly trying to put money in your pocket."

"Well, like they say, sister, sister, girlfriend, all money ain't good money."

"That's right. I forgot you and your husband got all kinds of money, especially when you have a flock of sheep that will pay their tithes and offerings to a damn church and then go home and sit in the dark or run an extension cord from their neighbor's house when the electricity gets cut off while you riding around here in a Range Rover and living in your $600,000 home in Alpharetta. I'm surprised you came down here to hang out with us po' folks."

"You don't know shit about our church or our congregation."

"Y'all lower your voices," Autumn interjected.

"Whatever, if she doesn't want to be a part of the organization, that's fine and she has that right, but she will not sit here and judge me like she's perfect."

"Alexis Nicole Harrington, you know good and well Mom did not raise us to do things like this."

"Like always, you want to bring Mom into something. Stop being a clone of her and be your own damn woman. And what your momma doesn't know won't hurt her."

"Lexi, Aubrey, STOP! Why are you starting this organization? Why would women want to join?" Autumn inquired.

"Like I said, men are going to cheat and women are going to cheat with them, so why not help women empower themselves once the relationship is over?"

"Really? Prostituting them for material gain is empowering?" Aubrey gasped.

"I'm not talking to you so be quiet; you've already told me how you feel. I don't need to hear anything else from you. Besides, you might want to get a side dude since the Right Reverend Bishop Joseph ain't hitting it right," I smirked.

"That is it! I am not listening to anymore of this foolishness. I'm leaving! I can't believe you would throw back in my face something I told you in private! Honey, you might not think much of yourself and your vagina, but I value mine and I wouldn't be somebody's side chick or dressed-up whore for all the riches in Babylon. Where is that waitress? Autumn, don't let Madam Alexis talk you into jumping on the express train to hell."

"Don't worry about the bill, I got it. Just consider it to be my tithes and offering to you," I declared. Aubrey's face turned bright red as she threw a fifty-dollar bill on the table and strutted off.

"Alexis."

"What?!"

"Don't snap at me. I like your idea and it sounds interesting, but I have Morgan to think about so I need some time to think it over."

"That is understandable. Please know I'm starting this organization with or without you or Aubrey," I said while signaling for the waitress to bring the check.

AUBREY

WHEN I ARRIVED AT PAPPADEUX on Jimmy Carter Blvd in Norcross, Lexi and Aubrey were already seated and drinking. They both had a Captain's Hurricane drink and was eating crab cakes and alligator. I don't know when they developed the taste for alligator, but they can keep that. My mouth watered thinking about the Jumbo Shrimp Brochette. I was starving and I couldn't wait to devour the char-grilled bacon-wrapped shrimp filled with Monterey Jack cheese with dirty rice on the side. Brunch started out good and then turned south when Madam Alexis revealed her plan to start an organization to help men cheat.

I was pissed when I threw the fifty dollar bill on the table and sped out of Pappadeux's parking lot. Alexis had a lot of nerve to come at me like that and put my business in the street. That's why I don't tell people shit. She doesn't know me...no one knows the real Aubrey. She has always been an outspoken know-it-all; that's probably why her and Mom bump heads all the time. It almost takes an act of Congress to get her to come to family dinners at our parents' house.

I will not be a part of her brothel. I don't care how she tried to disguise it. Whoring is whoring and I will not be a part of encouraging women to sell their bodies for money, clothes, and cars. I don't need another secret to add to my growing list; I have enough skeletons in my closet to fill a cemetery. I cannot count the number of men and women that I have sexed. If any of those affairs were exposed it would be the end of Kai and me. I'm afraid of how he would react. Lately people don't break up with you anymore; they just kill you. Every time you turn on the news somebody is killing their husband, wife, or significant other. It used to be just white folks killing, but black people have started killing too.

This world is crazy. More people need to see some sort of mental health professional. Although I go weekly I'm not sure how much it is helping me. I probably need to see a sex therapist for my sexual addictions. As hard as I try to control it I can't. I called Vanessa to relieve some stress. She answered the phone on the first ring like she had been waiting on my call all day. As soon as I heard her voice I lost interest and immediately tried to figure out of way to keep the call casual and not commit to hooking up. The first words out of her mouth sounded needy. "I'm surprised to hear from you."

"Why is that?" I asked.

"When you left church you said you were meeting your sisters at Pappadeux and I know when you and your sisters get together you lose track of time." *Is this bitch a timekeeper?* I don't answer to my husband and I damn sure am not answering to her.

"Well, I left early. Alexis and I had words."

"Oh no, honey, are you okay?"

"I will be."

"I can come over if you want to talk."

"No, thank you, this too will pass. I don't want to talk about it; it will just make me mad again."

"Well, I'm here if you need me." She sounded so sincere.

"Thanks, Ness. I'm not going to stay on the phone, I just called to say hi."

"Okay, were you thinking about me? I was thinking about you."

"That's nice. I have to go; I am getting ready to run into Publix and get some groceries."

"You have to get off the phone to go in the grocery store?"

"No, but I don't want to be one of those people walking around the store on their cell phone."

"What's going on, Bre? You never have time for me anymore. We haven't made love months and the last time we talked you hung up the phone. You barely speak at church. Is there someone else?"

"Vanessa, you do understand that I have a husband and you do too. I have a lot going on and I am not going to keep explaining my schedule to you every time I talk to you. If this relationship is not providing what you need, then you can walk away."

She sounded desperate when she responded, "No, Bre, I am not saying that. I miss you, I want to see you, spend time with you, and touch you. Let's go away for the weekend."

"Girl, I cannot go away for the weekend with you, especially if I didn't have time to go out of town with my family. I am tired of every time we talk you act needy. This shit is really getting to be bothersome."

"Wait?! Where is all this coming from? What did I do, Bre?"

"Nothing. You knew what this relationship was when you became a part of it. Now you are demanding more than I am able to give you. So I tell you what...this relationship is over."

Again, I didn't give Vanessa time to respond. I hung up the phone. Ending the relationship brought peace. It was as if a weight had been lifted off my shoulders. I felt free. Little did I know this newfound freedom would be short-lived.

VANESSA

I WISH I COULD PUT hands on that bitch! Aubrey makes me sick, spoiled rotten heffa. She has taken me for granted for the last time. I was at her beck and call. Confused slut. So she ended our relationship? I will not be the only one with hurt feelings. As God is my witness I will see to it that her perfect life comes crumbling down. I guess she forgot that you need to treat friends as if they will become enemies. This bitch has more problems than a math book and even more secrets.

AUTUMN

BRUNCH WITH LEXI AND BRE at Pappadeux was horrible. I know Bre was against the idea of Side Chicks Unite, but I needed some extra coins. I haven't received a raise since Pluto was a pup. I could be a poster child for side chicks. I have had more than my share of other women's sorry-ass pair of pants. I'm in with SC Unite and I will tell Lexi when we meet at Mayor's Park in Union City this evening.

I arrived at the park thirty minutes before Lexi, so I got a head start on my laps. I couldn't wait to tell her about my weekend with Kevin. I don't know why I am so weak when it comes to that man, but it's been awhile and besides I haven't known Jonathan that long. We talked on the phone every night and we've been to lunch a couple of times, but I'm not opening the cookie jar just yet.

I know Lexi is going to frown when I tell her I slept with Kevin. He is sorry as pond water, but the man is head doctor; he's the best in the game. On a scale from 1-10 he is a 55. He's married and still a slut; he done slept with half the world. All them heffas know I'm his crazy baby momma. I don't know why he mess with me, especially after I split his head with the weed whacker. When he lived in the barracks at Fort Sam Houston, I broke into his room and stole all the remote controls to his TVs and other electronic items. I don't even know why I did it I just felt like being spiteful.

Just as I was completing my first mile I saw Lexi's white Lexus turn the corner, so I waited for her at the start line. She stepped out of the car wearing dark grey leggings, a purple asymmetric t-shirt, she bought in

Jamaica, and grey Nike Air Max sneakers. In true Alexis fashion she was wearing sunglasses. I turned up my nose and said, "Did you come to work out or put on a fashion show?"

"I came to work out, but I'm not sweating," she said while giving me a hug.

"So, what's been going?" she asked.

"Girl, I did the stupidest shit this weekend. I'm just ashamed of myself."

"What you do now? Please don't tell me you were fighting again."

"I slept with my baby daddy."

"What?!"

"Yes, I am so mad at myself. Now he won't stop calling and he texts me late at night and early in the morning."

"Was the sex good?"

"Hell yeah! You would ask me that," I laughed.

"That's all that counts; if it was bad, then you should be mad." I busted out laughing. I expected her to say something smart or give me the side eye.

"I'm not talking to you," I joked.

"You brought it up. Hell, if it wasn't good, then you wasted your time and I would be mad for you. I thought you had a new boo anyway. What's going on with him?"

"Jonathan? Nothing yet. We've only been on a few dates. I can't give him the good good too fast. I don't want him to think I'm easy. I'm using the ninety-day rule."

"Girl, please, if all he wants is the cookie he will wait you out and after he gets it he will drop you like a bad habit."

"I know that is true; I just want true love, Lexi."

"So do I" Lexi said solemnly. I looked at my sister and I could see sadness in her eyes. I decided to lighten the mood.

"Lexi, you can count me in Side Chicks Unite," I said.

"Yeah" she squealed and gave me a high five.

ALEXIS

I WANTED TO PUNCH SOMETHING. The picture of my molester and his fat-ass wife on Instagram made me sick to my stomach. As hard as I try I can't forgive him. Why does he get to have a normal life? He has a wife and six kids while I'm scarred. A part of me wished someone would violate his cookie-stealing little fat-ass twin daughters like he did me. The other part prays for their protection and that they never experience what I did. I wanted to clown his high yellow fat ass in the comment section. It does my heart joy that light-skinned brothers went out of style in the nineties and haven't made a comeback. Every time I see his face I want to throw up and scream, "hide your little girls they are not safe."

In black families we keep secrets. It's taboo to tell family business, so no matter what happens you keep your mouth closed. Everything is so hush hush. Growing up I would hear my aunt say, "Keep those white folks out of our business because once they get in it it's hard to get them out." I wonder if I slapped the hell out of him at the family annual Christmas party if I would feel better.

I'm almost forty and still messed up. I can't keep a man or I end up sharing one. I don't trust men, so I play Inspector Gadget, and when you go looking for stuff you will find it that's how I found out Michael was cheating. He left me at his apartment when he went to work. I checked his Internet history and saw that he visited secure booking for the Marriott the day before. I called the hotel and asked for Michael Olfanse, I was shocked when the receptionist transferred me to his room. My heart dropped.

I threw on a pair of black yoga pants and a grey sweat shirt, grabbed the keys to my rental car, and drove over there. He was getting out of his car when I walked up to him. He looked like he had seen a ghost. He jeopardized our relationship for some random chick he met at a restaurant where we had dinner and the shit didn't work out. How is that for Karma? And now he's calling talking about he loves and misses me. "They say what don't break a nigga make a nigga." I'm broken and bitter and I want to hit cheating-ass men in their pockets.

I have a special place in my heart for side chicks. A lot of women who are or have been side chicks have been through something as a little girl. Some have self-esteem issues, some are still dealing with childhood or abandonment issues. Many grew up without their father. At the end of the day there is a wounded little girl inside of an adult who just wants love. A lot of men prey on that and use, lie, and abuse women who deep down inside are good women and will do anything for their sorry asses. Well, the tides are about to turn: if they want to play, then they need to pay.

Autumn agreed to join Side Chicks Unite, LLC. When she said, "Count me in Side Chicks Unite" I gave her a high-five and we immediately went into planning mode. We got to get the word out, so we can meet potential ladies and the sponsors to explain exactly what we do. I had to find a realtor and the perfect location. "After we find some women who are interested we need to have an informational session," I told Autumn.

"Where will we find them?" she asked.

"We can put an ad on Craigslist," I said.

"Girl, do people still answer those ads? Especially with all the killings."

"Hell, I don't know...We can use the internet. They have websites that help people cheat. We need to think outside the box. Do you have any ideas?" I asked.

"No...you got the idea from China. What do they do to bring the men and women together?"

"Oh hell, I didn't read that part. But, getting lying cheating men is easy."

"What are we going to do, just approach random women and say, 'Do you want to be a side chick?'"

"Really?" I said sarcastically. "We can use social media or maybe start a meet-up group. Don't worry, we will work it out," I assured her although I wasn't sure. "Have you talked to Aubrey?"

"No, I don't have anything to say to Miss High and Mighty."

"Lexi, you didn't have to put her and Kai's business in the streets."

"Child, please, you can miss with that. I ain't thinking about her or Kai."

"Not trying to change the subject. What is up with you and Xavier?"

"It's over."

"What happened!?"

"I don't want to discuss that right now...can we focus on SC Unite?" I owe the idea of organizing side chicks to all the Matthews, Michaels, and Xaviers of the world. Side Chicks Unite, LLC is not about the money - it's about revenge.

ALEXIS

I RENTED A TEMPORARY OFFICE for the meetings. Once I find an apartment complex I will use one of the apartments for our office. I looked at the time on my cell phone it was 7:30 pm, so I started the meeting. "Thank you, ladies, for your interest in Side Chicks Unite, LLC. I will explain the organization's goal and mission, as well as what it is and what it is not, and at the end of the presentation you will be able to ask questions." I said.

"How many women are in college or have been to college?" I asked. About five hands went up. I was not surprised; it was what I expected. Women are 33% more likely to have obtained a degree. College is the biggest rip-off. The sad part is people leave college owing more in student loans than they owe on their mortgage. It's a new form of slavery because you have to die to get away from it. To hell with Sallie Mae or Navient! SC Unite will start our own college fund and a portion of the proceeds from unfaithful men will go towards scholarships to deserving students. "I decided to start this organization because I've been involved with more married men than I can count. I can honestly say that I loved most and would have loved to be the next missus. It didn't work out that way and I ended up alone, heartbroken, and trying to pick up the pieces. After each affair I vowed I would never get involved with another married man - until the next one came along. I came to the conclusions that if men are going to cheat and have a side piece I might as well capitalize on it. The men will get what they want so they can better stay in unfulfilling relationships or whatever drives them to cheat. SC Unite - we don't wreck families. We keep them together by offering an escape. It's an expensive escape;

nevertheless, it is an escape. The men will go through a rigorous screening process to make sure they are mentally stable and can meet the financial terms of this organization. They will be required to pay all your living expenses, college tuition and other applicable fees," I explained. I could tell by the look in the women eyes they were interested.

"We will only choose women who are mentally sound, have attainable goals, and who can abide by the rules of this organization. If you are chosen I promise your life will be better. You will be required to sign a non-disclosure form." When I mentioned the non-disclosure form some of the women looked confused. "Let me reassure you that the non-disclosure form is for everyone's protection: you, the organization, and the men involved. The men are high-profile individuals such as athletes, entertainers, politicians, et cetera. When the relationship ends you will be financially secure." As I looked around at the diversity of women I could tell the ones who would not make it into the organization. We wanted women who were looking to come up for now and wanted love later. In China, a typical day for an ernai includes waking up, getting dressed, shopping, and visiting others in their apartment complex or village. The ernai's job is to keep her boyfriend company four or five nights per month. I'm not too keen on the women chilling at home every day and visiting each other this is not "The Real Side Chicks of Atlanta," I wanted the women to do something productive with their lives, do the things they always wanted to do but couldn't because they didn't have the money.

"We are not ladies of leisure and remember nothing lasts forever. This is your opportunity to come up, so use it wisely. You might accompany him to functions that will be at his and your discretion. Here are the basic rules: do not try to take the wife's place or you will be put out of the organization; avoid talking about his wife; respect his privacy and ensure that he does the same for you. I understand that you can't tell your heart how to feel, but I would guard my heart and try not to fall in love. If you feel this happening, please come and talk to me or Autumn. If he says he is falling in love with you let me know immediately. Do not get pregnant, and protect yourself from sexually-transmitted disease. Most likely you and his wife are not the only women in his life. The men chosen have a vested interest in their marriage and have something to lose. Again, if you are selected to join the organization under no circumstance can you tell anyone," I stated. All of us must be ready for any backlash if there is a fall-out. Side chicks get a bad rap they are said to have no morals. Most women swear they will never be a side chick, but many have been one and didn't even know it. People say that a side chick doesn't respect herself and has low self-esteem. I get so tired of hearing the line: "If I can't be number one, I will not be number two." And if I hear one more person say that you can't spend holidays with him because it's reserved for his family, I am going to scream. The saying that makes my skin crawl is when the side chick is called a "cum dumpster." We are not left-over trash. We have feelings. We want love. The other woman scares a lot of women because they can't stop the relationship. I looked at the room full of eager women and said, "Ladies, we are going to change the game. Are you ready?"

I found the perfect location for SC Unite in East Point. It was a three-story, twelve-unit multifamily complex. It was close to the Marta Station and just two miles south of the Fort McPherson and it was three miles west of the new Porsche North American Headquarters. Also, the current owners invested over $50,000 in rehabbing the place. It had new plumbing and electrical system; each unit had an alarm system and double-stacked washer/dryer. The cost was $550,000. I don't have that much in savings. I did not want a mortgage on this building, so I really needed an investor. I know that Autumn didn't have the money to put in. She is living paycheck to paycheck. Aubrey has the money to help; however, she thinks what we are doing is morally wrong. I haven't talked to Miss High and Mighty since the argument at Pappadeaux. I don't regret what I said, so I will not apologize for my beliefs. I stand in my own truth. I do miss her but I will not be judged. I'm going to live my life the way that I choose and if someone doesn't like it, oh well.

* * *

I really wanted this apartment complex. The neighborhood was not that great, but I think the City of East Point is trying to revitalize the area. I saw new businesses being built in the area. I don't want to rent apartments in another apartment community; I wanted to own the complex.

At first I thought about finding a spot in Buckhead, but with the money they are putting in South Atlanta I think this is the best move. I started looking for the men who would be sponsors of the side chicks. I posted ads in Craigslist and we started a Facebook page and a website. I figured if other sites like AshleyMadison.com or Cheaters Club can openly advertise, we can too. I was making a list of interview questions for the men when my phone rang.

"Hello?"

"Hi, may I speak to Alexis?"

"This is she," I say. I was concerned about my identity being found out with me being on the radio and everything. But, I must be at the forefront of the organization because it was my idea. Besides, I like to be hands-on and don't trust people to handle my business.

"My name is Todd and I saw your ad on Craigslist, and I would like some more information."

"I have an opening on Friday to discuss the organization, mission, goals, rules, and eligibility requirements," I responded.

"Friday is good. What time?"

"I have an opening at 3:00 pm and 7:00 pm."

"I can make it at seven o'clock. Is this a private session or group meeting?"

"This is a private meeting. It is our goal to protect the privacy and identities of our clients."

"Great! I will see you Friday at seven," Todd said.

"Ok, I have penciled you in for seven o'clock on Friday, look forward to meeting with you. Have a nice day," I replied. Todd's voice sounded familiar and for some reason I didn't believe that Todd was his real name. I would find out on Friday.

KAI

I MET DEIRDRE AT THE duck pond at Vander Veer Park. I always loved jogging around the park when I lived here. Dee was my first love; we met our junior year at Central High School. She was the new girl - she had just moved to the Quad Cities from Chicago. Dee had a tough-girl exterior but was the sweetest person once you got to know her and she let her guard down. She was smart and sassy and had the prettiest smile. I loved her shoulder-length hair. She was petite at 5'1" with a paper-brown complexion. I arrived at the duck pond before she did, so I let KJ drop bread crumbs in the water.

"What's up, K?" I turned around and looked and Dee was walking up pushing a stroller.

"What's going on, shorty?" I replied while giving her a hug. She hated when I called her shorty back in the day and the way she turned her lips up let me know she still wasn't fond of being called that.

"Just trying to make it," she said.

"I see you still looking good. Who is this precious little girl?" I asked.

Smiling, she said, "This is Kia...our daughter."

My mouth dropped. "Huh...our what?" I stuttered.

"You heard me, your daughter," she said. I thought back to my last visit when we met for drinks. We started reminiscing and one thing led to another, and the next day I woke up in her bed. I have carried that guilt for so long. I cheated on Aubrey and I had just became an ordained minister. I felt so bad that morning because my flesh was weak and now my indiscretions were coming back to haunt me. I could not deny Kia was my child - she looked just me and KJ. She was three months younger than KJ. In the hood we call that ghetto twins. I still wanted a DNA test and if the test showed that she was mine I would take care of her. I had to figure out how to tell Aubrey. *What would the church say? What would my family?* "Why are you just now telling me this?" I asked.

"Honestly, I was afraid you would want me to have an abortion."

"Why would you think that?"

"You were telling me how you and Aubrey had decided to have a baby and you went on about how much you loved her. The next day you left my apartment like your ass was on fire."

"True." I smiled. "Well, before I go back to Atlanta we need to do a DNA test."

"I am not a slut; I know who my baby daddy is. I hadn't had sex in over a year when we hooked up. K, you know me better than that."

"I know, Dee, but when I tell Aubrey she is going to want proof."

"The proof is that she looks just like your ass."

"Yes, she does. I still want the test. If the test shows she is mine, I will pay child support and I will be in her life. I want her to come to Atlanta to visit the whole nine."

"That sounds reasonable. How long are you going to be here?"

"A week."

"We can get it done on Monday," she said, and handed me my daughter.

AUTUMN

ALEXIS TOLD ME SHE FOUND an apartment complex in East Point not far from Fort McPherson. The only problem is we need more money. Alexis is so stubborn - she refused to call Aubrey so we could get some help with the financing. She knows that I don't have any money to invest. I live from check to check and with my credit score I couldn't get a loan for twenty-five cents. I felt bad that I couldn't contribute financially. We can't do everything by ourselves. We needed a team and some people with some money. Alexis tries to be an "Army of One." She will not ask for help. I keep telling her that team work makes the dream work. I have got to get Aubrey and Alexis talking again, and then maybe we can convince her to come on board and put money into something she thinks is a sin. I tried to think of the right words to say as I dialed Aubrey's number.

"Hello," Aubrey said.

She didn't sound like herself. "Hey, girl," I said. "Are you okay? You sound like you're sick."

"I'm good. Just tired," she whispered.

"Tired? What's going on?" I asked.

"Just working and trying to keep up with my little man."

"How's my nephew doing?"

"He's good. He is getting bigger by the day and he stays in everything. I can't take my eyes off him for a minute."

"Girl, you might need to put a bell on him."

"I will not put a bell on my baby like a dog."

"Lighten up, I'm just playing. Why are you so serious? You seem agitated. What's going on?"

"I'm tired, Dani. So much is happening. I really want my own TV show and most of all I miss hanging with my sisters.

"You seem stressed. Let's meet for lunch this week and have some spirits and just chat like old times."

"That would be great. What day and time?"

"Let's meet at Maggiano's at Cumberland Mall on Wednesday. How about one o'clock?"

"That's fine, I will see you Wednesday."

"Great! Kiss my nephew for me."

"I will, and give my niece a kiss for me."

"Ok. Bye, Bre Bear, I love you."

"OMG, don't call me that. I love you too, Dani. Bye."

I smiled as I pressed the end button. I didn't have the guts to tell her that Alexis would be there too. I was afraid she wouldn't come.

KAI

I RECEIVED THE RESULTS FROM the DNA test a week after I returned home and the results revealed that Kia is mine. I wasn't surprised; she looked just like me. I would take responsibility for my indiscretions. I wanted Kia and KJ to know each other, so I don't have a choice but to tell Aubrey. Then I will have to explain to the church and if they want me to step down, so be it. I love Aubrey and would be devastated if she left. I hope we can get through this, but I will not deny my child. I am going to be in her life. No one is perfect and we all fall short. I picked up my cell phone and called Dee; she answered on the first ring. "I guess you got the test results?" she said. No hello, just straight to the point. "Yes, I did" I replied.

"So, what do we do now?" she asked.

"I guess we have to figure this out. I want to be a part of my child's life and I will take care of her."

"That's good to know. I want Kia to know her father and her brother."

"And her step-mother."

"Oh, so you told your wife?"

"Not yet. I am going to tell her this evening. I just wanted to touch base with you and let you know that I received the results, so we can decide how we are going to co-parent."

Dee and I agreed that we would not go to court for a child support order; I would pay her $1000 a month plus I would pay for child care expenses. After I hung up with Dee it was time for me to face the music and let my green-eyed wife know what I had done. I was apprehensive - this woman has a temper and I didn't want this argument to escalate, especially with KJ in the next room napping.

I walked into the kitchen and as usual Bre was cleaning and rearranging the items in the cabinet. *I swear, nothing can be unorganized or out of place with her.* This was the hardest thing I ever had to do. I took a deep breath and said, "Honey, do you have a minute to talk?" She put the neatly stacked plastic bowls in the lower cabinet and said, "Sure." I took a seat on the bar stool at the island. I looked in her eyes and I tried to speak but the words would not come. I saw the worry in her eyes as she sat down next to me and said, "Kai, what's wrong?"

I started with the corny line, "You know that I love you and I would never do anything to intentionally hurt you." I couldn't look her in the eyes. I looked down. She lifted my chin and looked me straight in the eyes and said, "Just say whatever you need to say."

"I have a child...a little girl. Her name is Kia Janae."

Bre took her hand off my face and said, "Child?"

"Yes, I just found out that I have a daughter in Davenport by an old girlfriend."

"Are you sure she is yours?"

"Yes, I took a paternity test and the result revealed that she is my child." I handed her the DNA results.

"How old is she?" she asked.

"Six months," I said. I looked in her eyes and saw the hurt.

"Six months!?"

"I'm sorry, Bre. Let me explain." I told her what happened when I went to Davenport - how Dee and I had drinks and the next day I woke up in her apartment in her bed naked. I could see her fighting back the tears. I explained to her the arrangement that Dee and I made and how much child support I was going to pay for Kia. I told her that Kia would come and visit regularly because I wanted her to know who we were and to be a part of our family. I assured her that I loved her and KJ with all my heart and nothing had changed. I apologized profusely for my infidelity in the relationship and swore that it only happened the one time and that it would never happen again. She got up from the barstool, walked to the refrigerator, and poured wine into a glass. She sounded hurt when she asked, "Where do we go from here?"

"I don't want to lose you. I want us to stay married. I know this is hard, so I was thinking we could go to counseling." She picked up her glass of wine and walked out of the kitchen.

AUBREY

KAI'S CONFESSION OF HIS INFIDELITY in our marriage caught me off-guard. I would have never thought in a million years that the saved and sanctified Bishop Joseph would cheat and be so stupid to make a baby. I held my tears in - I refused to let him see me cry. When I walked out of the kitchen my emotions betrayed me and tears flowed down my face like a dam had burst. I hurried to the guest bathroom, my legs wobbling as I sat on the side of the bathtub. My stomach fluttered, my heart hurt so bad it felt as if I had a ton of bricks lying on my chest. Kai tapped lightly on the bathroom door. I didn't answer. I couldn't talk to him. I knew I would go off and I didn't want to scare KJ.

Honestly, I couldn't be mad at Kai - I had cheated with more men and women that I could count. I guess I felt like I was better than him because I never got caught. But, I was no better than him. If the child was a few years older than KJ I could understand, but this woman and I were pregnant at the same time. I didn't bother to ask her name. I'm sure it was Deidre. I knew they dated in high school and she was his first true love. If I stayed I would accept the child. She didn't ask to come here.

I didn't know if I could stay. I needed to see Dr. J and talk about this as soon as possible. It's times like this when I needed to talk to my big sister Lexi. I felt so alone, like I didn't have anyone in the world to talk to. I used to confide in Vanessa. Now when I see her at church I refused to make eye contact with her; this way I didn't have to speak.

I have tried to be the perfect wife, mother, daughter, and sister, all while hiding my secrets. I'm tired of secrets. I am looking forward to lunch with Autumn on Wednesday and I know Alexis will be there even though Autumn failed to say it. Those two are like peas in a pod. I know my baby sister wants us to kiss and make up and so do I.

I splashed water on my face, dried it, and walked out of the bathroom. I walked back into the kitchen. Kai was holding KJ. He looked at me when I walked in and smiled weakly. KJ got out of his lap and walked to me. I picked my baby up and hugged him so tight that he started wiggling. I handed him back to Kai and sat down. "I'm not going to counseling."

Kai put KJ in the high chair and said, "Okay."

"I don't know how we are going to fix this or if this marriage is worth salvaging."

"Of course it is, Bre. I made a mistake. I've let everyone down. I don't care what anyone else thinks. I just want you and KJ to be a part of Kia's life." His eyes showed he was sincere. I knew he was telling the truth; however, I couldn't give in that easy.

I've been through this before with Christopher and he broke my heart numerous times, every time I would forgive him he'd promised he would never do it again until he got caught with the next random chick. After that relationship I vowed that I would never stay in a relationship with a cheating man, because if he did it once he would do it again. He has a baby with this woman so most likely he can always have sex with her. That seemed to be the pattern with Christopher and his four baby mommas. This is one of the reasons why I never completely give my heart to one person, hence the affairs. I am always careful; I've never been caught. How could he be so careless? What if he got more than a daughter? How was he going to explain a sexually transmitted disease? This bastard was lucky all he got was a child. I have to make an appointment to have an HIV/AIDS test as soon as possible. I poured another glass of wine and said, "I'm going to stay in a hotel for a while and I'm taking my son."

ALEXIS

I KNEW THAT TODD'S VOICE sounded familiar, but when he walked in my office I was surprised to see Congressman Jason Todd Carey. He had smooth chocolate skin, stood about 6'0" tall; his hair was tapered on the sides and back and curly at the top. He was the last person I expected to see in my office. I knew that he had been with his wife Marian since he was in law school and she helped him to get to where he was in politics. Marian's family had money, whereas Jason's family had none. I guess the family wasn't as happy as they look in the media and on social media websites. My my my, could there be trouble in paradise or is he one of those men who just liked to get a little piece on the side?

It doesn't make me any difference as long as he meets the income requirements, passes all the other tests, and his money comes in on time. After shaking my hand he did not sit down. He walked around looking at the art on the wall and pacing back and forth. He started to make me nervous. So I said, "Congressman Carey, please have a seat," while pointing to the chair at the small conference table.

"Thank you," he replied and pulled out a chair. I removed the white and grey flower vase from the center of the table, so we could have more room to go over the forms. I wanted him to be comfortable and sitting at the small round conference table was a little more informal. *I swear, this brother is finnne!* If I hadn't given up being a side chick I would keep him for myself.

I explained the rules of the organization. I told him that the women have strict rules and if they break those rules they would be released from the organization, and that everyone is required to sign a non-disclosure form. I assured him that our goal was to make sure that his identity would be completely confidential; however, there were risks because nothing is 100 percent guaranteed. But we would do our best. *I still had to get the funding for the apartment complex.* Congressman Carey must have noticed that I was deep in thought because he asked, "Are you okay?"

"Yes, I'm sorry" I replied. "I was thinking about all the things I have to do," I added.

"I understand; sometimes my mind wanders," he laughed. "Can you tell me about the security of my information? How will the data collected be used?" he asked.

"All information will be kept on an external drive, which will be locked in a vaulted safe. We ask about financial information to ensure that you will be able to provide the lifestyle for the woman you get involved with."

"What about my health information? What is it used for?"

"We want to make sure that you are healthy and that you are mentally sound. We do the same health and mental health assessment on the women. Our goal is to protect everyone involved. You will be assigned a number that will correlate with a pseudo name, only I will know everyone's true identity."

"How will the physical exam and lab work be conducted? Is there a doctor on staff?"

"No, we do not have a doctor on staff to complete the physical. You can have your family physician complete the physical and any lab work and bring the results back to me. As far as the mental health assessment, you will complete the questionnaire and bring it back to me. At that time you will be assigned a number, and a licensed clinical psychologist will evaluate your answers. If everything is fine, you will get to see profiles of the women, you choose one, and then I will arrange a meeting."

"What if I choose a woman and it doesn't work out? Do I have to keep her?"

Laughing, I said, "Of course not." He smiled at me with his eyes. I could tell he wanted to say something else. So I said, "Is there anything else you would like to know?"

"Yes, would you like me to take the forms home and bring them back with the results from my physical, or fill them out here?"

"It doesn't matter; it's up to you. You can do whatever makes you feel comfortable."

"I'll fill them out and bring them back. This will give me a chance to really think about if this is something I want to do."

"That is fine; please take your time and decide. There is no hurry because it is a risk as well as a financial commitment."

"Are you one of the women that I could possibly be hooked up with?" He asked. I bit my bottom lip and smiled. "Sorry, but I am not on the menu." I could feel myself blushing as thoughts of what I could do with this man ran through my head. I just got out of a relationship with a married man and I was tired of being number two. I felt like a hypocrite because here I was starting an organization to help married men cheat on their wives and yet I did not want to be cheated on. I've had my share of married unavailable men. I want a man of my own...a family...true love. I watched him as he walked to the door.

He turned the door knob and looked back at me and said, "That's too bad. I really want you to be my girlfriend."

AUTUMN

I AM SUPER AMPED THAT my sisters and I will be together again. I truly missed us laughing and cutting up. Alexis and I arrived at Maggiano's at the same time. I tried to arrive before her so I could get a table for three. She valeted her car, so she was waiting for me at the entrance to Maggiano's. I could park my car myself and walk. I needed to save my coins. "Can you seat us at a large booth or table?" I asked the hostess. Alexis looked at me strangely. "What?" I said.

"Why a large booth or table?"

"Because I'm hungry and I need some elbow room," I whispered while following the hostess to our table. I didn't plan on going back to work so I was definitely having a glass of wine or two. They made my nerves bad today with all the gossiping and negative energy. I hoped that Aubrey showed up and more importantly that she would help us with the funding for SC Unite. As soon as we were seated I said, "Please bring me a glass of Moscato."

"You must not be going back to work."

"Nope. My nerves are bad. I can't deal with those people today."

"I'll have a glass, too," Alexis said. "Better yet, just bring us a bottle. Thank you." I looked at Lexi. I could tell she had a lot on her mind. She is the oldest and always tries to be the strongest. I have told her many times to let her emotions out before she goes off and kills someone. I know like me, my sister desires love - true love. It seems that every time she finds Mr. Right he turns out to be Mr. Wrong. I would say that it runs in the family, but it seems Aubrey found the perfect guy and this gives me hope. I looked up from the menu and I saw Aubrey walking towards us like she was on the runway. When she walked up to the table she didn't seemed surprised to see Alexis. I stood up and gave her a hug and kiss on the cheek and said, "Hey, big sister."

"Hello, Autumn," Aubrey smiled. I felt the cold stare from Alexis' hazel eyes burn my neck. I turned around, sat down, and avoided making eye contact with her. Aubrey slid in the booth next to me and greeted Alexis coldly.

I shook my head in disgust. "You two need to stop this foolishness!" I said, slightly above a whisper. "We grew up together and came from the same womb. Enough is enough, ladies." Suddenly Alexis got up and embraced Aubrey. "I'm sorry," she said.

"I'm sorry too, Lexi." Alexis signaled for the waiter to bring us another wine glass. The tension dissipated. After the waiter brought a wine glass for Autumn I proposed a toast. "To the Harrington sisters... family is all we got." We clinked glass and started catching up. So much had happened since we had brunch. While sharing chicken sausage and Italian sausage flatbread Aubrey revealed that Kai had a six-month-old daughter. I almost flat-lined at this news. I could hear the hurt in my sister's voice as she told us about Kai's cheating with his high school sweetheart while visiting his hometown in Iowa. I felt as hurt as she did. I looked up to them; their relationship gave me hope and this news shattered my hopes.

When Aubrey finished talking you could hear a rat piss on cotton. I broke the silence by saying, "Bre Bear, I am so sorry this happened to you. It really sucks to be cheated on and what's worst he made a baby. I am here for you if you need to talk." I looked at Alexis and I could see her eyes change colors from hazel to dark brown - this could only mean one thing: she was pissed.

Alexis said, "Aubrey, I am so sorry. Like Autumn said, we are here for you. I apologize for the hurtful things I said to you. Although we can't erase the pain, please know we will help you get through this."

"Thank you so much. I really need my family...my sisters right now."

"I know how you feel. I have been through this with Morgan's father. This too shall pass; you just got to go through it."

"I have been through this too," Alexis said. Aubrey and I looked at her in disbelief. "Yes, I was pregnant by Marquise and he got this chick named Annette pregnant. I lost my baby because he threw me out of a moving car and she had his son." My stomach churned I could no longer eat. I kept sipping my wine. I had no idea that my sister had been through something like that and never shared her experience with anyone. Alexis looked at Aubrey and said, "I have been through so much with men that I'm surprised that I am still alive. I keep telling myself that I am not a victim. I am a survivor. I know you think me starting SC Unite is about money and material gain. I know you think that it is evil and a sin. I am bitter and I want revenge."

Aubrey looked at Alexis and said, "I understand, but two wrongs don't make it right. We all have baggage and have been damaged. We are all survivors of something...some unfortunate event in our life." Alexis turned her head. "Wait, Lexi!" Aubrey said. "I am not judging your motives; I'm just putting it out there. I understand your pain and I want revenge too. So, all I can say is 'Side Chicks Unite!'"

ALEXIS

I WAS NOT SURPRISED WHEN Aubrey arrived at Maggiano's. I knew Autumn invited her in order to get us to kiss and make-up. I'm glad she did. I missed hanging out with my sisters; they are the best in the world. I was stunned to find out about Kai's infidelity. Men can be so stupid. I guess they haven't heard of condoms or at a minimum pulling out. I guess the Harrington sisters have had our share of relationship challenges.

People think that because you are beautiful, pretty, or attractive that men will not cheat on you. Good looks don't make you immune from a cheating man. So often women beat themselves up when they get cheated on - they wonder what is wrong with them? What could they have done to prevent it from happening? How can they change so it will not happen again? When a person chooses to cheat, whether man or woman, it says more about their character than the person they cheated on. You would think when a person gets to be in their forties or fifties they would know what they want - many don't. It's a shame that people are so afraid of growing old, so they try to hold on to their youth by doing stupid shit. I keep telling people the only alternative to not getting older is dying. It sickens me when a man over fifty is still trying to be a player. He needs to get his old ass somewhere and sit down and try to get closer to God.

There is nothing wrong with a single man or divorced man weighing his options, but don't tell a woman that she is the only one and then go off and cheat with another woman; just be a man about it and tell the truth. When Michael and I talked after our confrontation in the parking lot at the Marriott, I told him that his lying took away my options and if he wanted to see other women he should have been truthful because if he was going to date other women then I was going to date other men. He damn sure wasn't going to be the only one dating. He was busted and still tried to lie. I've heard men say: that if a man really loves a woman if he gets caught cheating he will not admit to it because he is trying to protect her. That doesn't make me feel better and it damn sure doesn't make me feel loved or protected.

I couldn't stop looking at the cashier's check that Aubrey gave me for $300,000 - and she agreed to do all the decorating. This check, along with the money I have, will cover the cost of buying the apartment complex in East Point. Having Aubrey join SC Unite is wonderful. At last the Harrington sisters will be working together. We are about to change the game. We each have our own motivation and that is what will fuel this train.

AUBREY

IT FELT SO LIBERATING TO tell my sisters about Kai's cheating and his baby girl. It was much cheaper than seeing Dr. J. Alexis revealing that she was pushed out of a moving car and lost her baby was shocking. I guess we all have secrets. I swear, black folks are the gurus of keeping secrets; especially family secrets. It felt good to give Alexis $300,000 of Kai's money to buy the apartment complex. Well actually it's his church's money. I transferred the money from one of the church's account to my personal account. All I can say is look at God, won't he do it.

I know that I will get my money back quickly because men love to get a little ass on the side. *Oh well, I just added another secret to my repertoire.* Alexis' ring tone interrupted my thoughts. "Hey girl," I said.

"Hey, sis," she replied.

"What's up?"

"Not too much. I was calling to say thank you again for investing in SC Unite. I know it goes against your morals and principles." "You're welcome and don't worry about my morals and principles. It's all good."

"I know we are going to make a lot of money and you will get your $300,000 back hopefully within a year."

"I'm not worried, but technically it's not my money. It belongs to the Lord." I was tired of keeping secrets so I decided to be honest with my sister.

"Huh?"

"Like Daddy says, if you can huh, you can hear," I laughed.

"Bre, what do you mean it's the Lord's money?"

"Just what I said. I borrowed the money from the church, so if they get it back they do and if they don't they don't. Lord help those who help themselves."

"Bre, I don't know about this."

"Did you cash the check?"

"Yes."

"Then it's done. Look at God...won't He do it?"

"Will he won't." Alexis laughed while speaking in tongue. I joined in, and for some strange reason I didn't feel bad borrowing money from the church. Hell, if people are willing to buy private jets for their bishop, then buying an apartment complex for the less fortunate shouldn't trouble their spirit.

"I was calling to see if you wanted to go with me to look at the apartment building. I spoke with the realtor and he is going to meet me there in an hour."

"Sure, I was just leaving from getting a pedicure." I lied. I had just left Dr. J's office and this time there wasn't a whole lot of talking going on. It started out professionally - he started the session with me doing EFT, which is short for Emotional Freedom Technique, to help me balance my energy, and the next thing I know we're having sex on his sofa. He wasn't all that great. I still had a happy ending, so it's all good. "Text me the address, I'm in Midtown so it shouldn't take me long to get there. The traffic is not bad on 75/85S just yet."

"Okay, I'm sending it to you now. See you in a few."

"All righty then...oh, is Autumn coming?"

"Yes."

"Ok," I responded. I pressed "end" on my Galaxy S6 edge and headed south in my Range Rover.

VANESSA

I PUT A SPYWARE PROGRAM on Aubrey's Surface Pro3 while she was sleeping after one of our rendezvous. I must admit she was smart. Most of the things on her Surface Pro were work-related, mostly different design elements. She didn't have any financial records or client information. I know she kept all that information on her home computer. She decorated the homes of some rich and famous people so she was always cautious about protecting her clients' information.

I got lucky when I logged into her personal bank account and noticed a $300,000 transfer from a church account to her personal account. Then I noticed that a cashier check for the same amount was issued. I wonder what would make her steal from the church. I guess the saying is true: if you cheat you will steal and if you steal you will kill. Later I will call the bank and pretend to be her so I can find out if the check had been cashed and by who, but in the meantime this message should put little Mrs. American Top Model on high alert. I texted her: "Thou Shalt Not Steal."

ALEXIS

WHEN MY SISTERS AND I walked into the apartment complex I could tell they were impressed. "This is like going from hell to heaven," Aubrey said. I knew exactly what she meant. The outside of the building was nice, but the neighborhood looked run-down. "Maybe it will look better when the sun is shining," Autumn joked. It was an overcast day and it had been raining and drizzling all day and this made the neighborhood look a little more rundown and depressing.

"Right," I snickered as we walked into the first apartment.

"Listen, there is nothing set in stone that we have to buy this property. I have a plan B," I stated. Bre looked at me and said, "I know you have a plan B, C, D, EFG, Alexis. Let's just do a walk-through."

"I agree," Autumn uttered. We went through each apartment and talked about style and decorating choices. Aubrey was in her element when we talked about decorating each unit. Suddenly, I had an epiphany.

"The women can decorate their unit to fit their style and their sponsor can pay for it. Of course, they will have to use Aubrey's company; this way we can keep the money circulating in the organization."

"I like how you think, big sister!" Autumn exclaimed.

I smiled at my brilliant thought. "I said we were going to change the game. Game on, bitches," I whispered. I didn't want, Curtis, the realtor to hear our business.

"So, how do you ladies like the property?" Curtis asked.

"It's nice. It needs very little work, so that's great."

"Are you ladies prepared to make an offer?" he inquired.

"Can you give me and my sisters a minute to talk in private?" I responded.

"Sure, take all the time you need," he replied. We strolled into the kitchen and huddled. "So what do y'all think?" I asked.

"I like it."

"Me, too," Aubrey added.

"Do you want to make an offer or do you want to rent spaces in another apartment complex?"

"Hell no, this is rental property. The men will pay the rent for their 'second wife.' It's all about making money."

"So we are in agreement then. We are going to buy this property."

"Hell yeah," my sisters said in unison as we high-fived each other. We walked back to Curtis and I said, "We are ready to make an offer for $450,000, all cash."

The bank countered our offer at $495,000, we accepted, and we were in business. After closing, my sisters and I went to Aubrey's hotel room to celebrate and to select the side chicks for SC Unite. We looked at the photos, profiles, and health records of each woman and carefully handpicked each side chick. By the end of the night and three bottles of Moscato we had narrowed it down to six women out of more than fifty prospects. We chose Shamika Matthews, Sia Jones, Sydni Butler, Deborah Davis, Ebony Taylor, and Shawnee Moore.

We were using one unit for our office and one would be for security, so we had ten apartments available. We still had four apartments that needed to be filled because an empty apartment is a loss of money, but I would rather lose money than put some woman in it who cannot abide by the rules.

As the leader I must protect everyone. We all had something at stake. We looked at the women's pictures again to make sure that we were in agreement; there was something about Shamika and Sia that I liked. They came to the meeting together. Their applications stated that they were students at Georgia State University. Shamika was 5'3" with a huge personality she was from a small town and was determined to live a life different from how she grew up. I could tell she was driven by material things and that was fine with me as long as she followed the Side Chicks Commandments. She wore an expensive weave, green contacts, and designer clothes. She seemed to be high maintenance. I liked when she said, "I don't give my cookie to just anyone. I have good credit and 401K cookie." It was hard for me to contain my laughter; however, this let me know that she was driven by money. Her favorite saying was, "the dream is free; the hustle is sold separately." She came from a large family and was adamant that she was not going to be a baby factory like her mother.

I was concerned about Sia; she was model-esque with a caramel-brown complexion and long straight thin hair - just drop-dead gorgeous. She was an only child and came from a single-parent home. During the interview she expressed the sadness of not having her father in her life. What I have learned from some women who did not have a relationship with their father that often they looked for him in other men. She revealed that she eventually wanted to be married and have children. This concerned me because I didn't want the lines to be blurred with her sponsor. There is nothing wrong with wanting a family - hell, I want one too - but you can't make someone else's family your family. Of all the prospects these two stood out the most. The rest of the women were smart, pretty, and driven but they didn't have the "it" factor that these two had. It was no wonder they were best friends.

"So, where do we get the men?" Aubrey asked.

"I've interviewed some potential sponsors. I am waiting for all their paperwork to come back," I said while showing them a list of names.

"Paperwork? What paperwork?" Aubrey asked.

"Oh, they have to go through the same screening process as the women: they must bring me back the result of their physical, HIV/AIDS test and other test for sexually transmitted diseases, and fill out a mental health questionnaire that will be analyzed by a reputable psychologist. Also, they must provide financial information. We have income guidelines, darling."

"What if the results of the physical has been tampered with?" Autumn inquired.

"I have to go on their word, but we can add something to their contract that will hold them liable for any false statements on their application."

"Wow, you have thought of everything," Aubrey remarked.

"No, I haven't. That why I need y'all's input or suggestions in case I forgot something."

"Well, have you thought about how to protect the identity of the side chicks and the sponsors? I mean with the hackers getting the information from that cheating website, the sponsors are going to want assurance that their identity and information are protected," Aubrey said.

I was starting to feel tipsy from the wine. I took another sip and replied,

"Why, yes I have, my dear sisters."

Looking at me side-eye Autumn said, "Let's hear it."

"I have an external hard drive that will have all of their information on it, which will be kept in a locked safe. Nothing will ever be stored on a laptop or personal computer. Once the organization is up and running I will put the external drive in a safe deposit box. I will use a different hard drive that will have only pertinent information for financial record-keeping. This information will be coded and each sponsor will be assigned a letter number code, but their real names will never be used."

Both of my sisters looked at me in disbelief. "Damn, you have thought of everything," Aubrey exclaimed.

"Not everything - just the basics and we can adjust as we see fit. For now let's look at the Side Chicks Commandments," I said as I pulled out a sheet of paper with the rules.

Side Chicks Unite Commandments

1. Thou shalt not steal husbands; thou can borrow him for a while.
2. Thou shalt not ruin the marriage.
3. Thou shalt enrich and enliven marriages.
4. Thou shalt not encourage him to leave his wife.
5. Thou shalt not take on the wife/main chick responsibilities.
6. Thou shalt not contact his wife.
7. Thou shalt always have protected sex.
8. Thou shalt not get pregnant.
9. Thou shalt not demand to be a priority.
10. Thou shalt remember your place and play your position...stay in your lane.
11. Thou shalt not call or text at obscene hours.
12. Thou shalt not post comments to his page on social media with sexual overtones.
13. Thou shalt practice discretion.

SHAMIKA

ROMANCE WITHOUT FINANCE IS NONSENSE. The cookie doesn't come out of the jar for just any sorry-ass man with a line, anymore. I have wasted so much time on romance, wanting love from a man, when I should have been focused on myself. I grew up poor and I hated it. Both of my parents worked and did the best they could to care for me and my five sisters and brother. Seeing how hard my parents worked and could barely make ends meet I was determined not to have that type of life. I watched my siblings follow the same path as my parents: get married, get a job, and go to work, home, and church. Many of them had a house of kids just like our parents.

When Sia told me about the meeting at Side Chicks Unite I was intrigued, but Alexis' pitch sold me. I have had my share of married men, some who provided for me financially and others who wanted me to be just a piece of ass on the side. Alexis assuring us that being a part of SC Unite we would come up financially - I was all in. I refused to be like two of my sisters who have degrees, work in unfulfilling jobs and are slaves to student loans. I want to travel the world, stay in five star hotels, and wear the finest clothes and shoes. I love shoes and handbags and I want to be able to buy any name-brand that I want.

I refuse to work all my life to make some company's CEO rich; I have an entrepreneurial spirit. I will be the CEO of my own company, so I can travel when I want. My first year in college I got involved with a much older man - Lawson Taylor. He gave me money and bought me whatever I wanted, but I got tired of him having to cancel our dates. It was so frustrating; I knew slaves who had more freedom than him. The last time he called he was in his feelings because I refused to meet up with him without him giving me some money. He had the nerve to say, "You used to be so innocent, but now you be on some other shit." He didn't want to give me money for my time. He can miss me with that; you have to play to pay when you are married. I'm so glad he's out of my life; all he did was tell lies. Like Mama would say, "He will tell a lie faster than a cat can lick its ass." That was Lawson - a well-dressed liar. He must have believed putting on them fancy suits would hide the fact that he was a pathological liar. The day I found out he was seeing me and some chick in my dorm I went off. I was sharing him with his wife, but I refused to share with another chick too. He tried to cover it up by saying he was helping her out because she was in school. Hell, I was in school too. He was always hemming and hawing whenever I asked for money. This goofy bastard was a trick daddy on a budget.

When I couldn't put up with the lies anymore I ended the relationship and on the rebound I met Tony. If I had known that Tony was a sorry lazy momma's boy I would have never given him the time of day. After three months of dating, I let Tony move in with me in my small one-bedroom apartment. I thought I would have someone to split the bills with. I was wrong. First of all, I should have saw the red flag when he was administratively withdrawn from school because he was behind on his tuition. I had no idea that he had been on academic probation for two semesters. I couldn't see past the mind-blowing sex and having someone to cuddle with at night. I was so happy to have a man that anything with a pulse would do. He could not keep a job and when he got fired it was never his fault. He was so negative about everything. It got to the point where I hated to come home and I was paying all the bills.

I remember when I took him home with me one weekend to meet my parents. I'll never forget the look on his face when I introduced him to my father and my father told him that if he put his hands on me he would kill him and preach over his funeral. I loved my father; he let the guys I dated know that I had a father and didn't need another one.

One thing I learned from my experience with Tony is that finances will strain a relationship; you cannot live off love. Love don't pay the bills. I was worried about how I was going to pay the bills and Tony was sitting his ass up in my apartment all day without a reason to get dressed. After all I've been through, SC Unite seemed like the perfect adventure for me.

The interview process was interesting. This was the first step in being accepted into the organization. The first question Alexis asked was, "What is your experience with cheating?"

"I believe that you cheat on them before they cheat on you" I answered. Alexis asked me why I felt this way and I replied, "Men cheat because they can and there is more opportunity for them to cheat since there are more women who are willing to sleep with a married man or a man already in a relationship."

I was shocked that one of the women in the group said that it's the woman's fault that men cheat because they don't honor their role as a wife. She got life fucked up if she thinks that it's the woman's fault if her husband cheats. My parents have been married for over forty years and my father cheated on her, and from what I saw my mother was a good wife. She worked every day and when she got home she cooked. My father gave her his check on Fridays and she made sure the bills were paid. We didn't have name-brand clothing, but we had clean clothes and we never went to bed hungry. My mother catered to my father's every need: she fixed his plate, ironed his clothes, and anything else that my father wanted my mother did. My mother was very submissive to my father. We just found out a year ago that my father had another son. My mom was hurt. This will not be my story.

ALEXIS

Operation Side Chick Unite was underway. We handpicked six women. We still needed four more, so I put Autumn in charge of recruiting the women. "I might take one of the spots." Autumn joked. "Girl, boo." I said.

"What?"

"You can't be one of the side chicks and be a business partner in the organization."

"Hell, I need some assistance," Autumn laughed.

"We pay you a salary, so stop clowning and look for some more women." With just the six girls we earned enough money to pay all our expenses to run the organization. Word of mouth is the best form of advertisement; I had so many requests from men who were willing to pay to have a fling on the side it made my head spin.

It's a damn shame that men ain't shit, I thought. Shamika and Sia had so many requests that they drove the administrative fees up. Hell, 401K booty cost more than EBT booty. I knew that Jason would want Shamika and I felt kind of jealous and I was not sure why. I did turn him down, after all. He was still trying to get with me. To be such a powerful man he had no chill. He busted out laughing when I said, "If you can't be with the one you want be with the one you can get with." When I introduced Jason to Shamika he looked at her like she was a piece of cake. I smiled when he gave me the thumbs-up. I knew that they would hit it off; based on their profiles they were a good match. They had a lot of the same interests. After their first dinner date Jason was hooked. The next day he signed the contract and paid the administrative fees.

However, being the dog that he was he was still trying to date me. Like most men he wanted to have his cake and to eat it, too. I must admit there was a strong attraction to Jason and I knew in my heart that a young girl like Shamika couldn't handle a man like Jason. Shamika was stoked about Jason being her sponsor. She knew he had money and power. When she was picking out the furniture and accessories for her apartment she was like a little kid at Christmas. "Thank you so much, Ms. Alexis, for choosing me to be in the organization," she said.

"You are welcome, but please just call me Alexis. Calling me miss makes me feel old." I hugged her and I said, "Welcome to the family."

"I apologize, Ms....I mean, Alexis. It's just that I'm from the South and I was taught to address an adult by Ms. or Mr."

"I know, it's a southern thing and it's all about respect. I'm from the Midwest and I wasn't raised that way, but we still had to respect adults. We had to say please, thank you, and excuse me and all the other polite respectful things when addressing others. We couldn't say yeah or naw to an adult. If an adult asked you a question we couldn't shrug our shoulder," I laughed. I looked at Shamika, all wide-eyed and ready for the world and said, "I am here for you. If you need to talk about anything please feel free to come to me. I know you and Sia are close and confide in each, but just know that I am here for you too."

"Thank you, Alexis, I appreciate it."

I smiled and said, "Again, welcome to the family."

When Aubrey walked in I immediately let her take over helping Shamika with her design choices for her apartment. Although I like decorating I have my limits and my patience is short, and I had to arrange a meeting to get all the girls together for their finishing classes. All the women in SC Unite will have social grace; they will be taught to speak eloquently, have etiquette, and develop true self-confidence. I don't want them to be the loud over-the-top designer clothes-wearing and purse-toting hoochies. When they are out in public they are a reflection of not just themselves, but the organization. Men are not the brightest stars in the sky and they just might take their side chick to an event. Knowing how many men think, they might even introduce them to some of their friends and family members. I know I have met more than my share of past lovers' family and friends and often they liked me more than the wife or main chick, or at least they pretended to. This doesn't concern me any; as long as everyone adheres to the rules of this organization and the men continually meet their financial obligation, they can get it how they live. Besides, when they leave the organization they will be refined women who will be able to dominate in the boardroom or be the CEO of their own company or whatever their heart desire. Society will not agree with what we are doing. I don't care; like I said before mistresses and concubines have been around since Biblical times.

When the rest of the ladies finished moving into their apartments we had our first meeting. I felt torn about what I was doing: on one hand I felt like I was empowering them because they would be taken care of by cheating dog-ass men, but on the other hand I felt like a madam. I had read each woman's profile many times; I knew the women who wanted true love and who had been hurt repeatedly by men. Then there were a couple here like me who had been molested as a child by a relative. Out of the six young ladies only two had a real relationship with their father, so they had a healthy image of what a man should and should not do to a woman.

In our own way each and every woman in the room was damaged and had to find a way to navigate through this thing we call life. I just hoped that I did more good than harm. After Autumn finished pouring champagne in everyone's glasses I raised my glass and said, "Welcome to the family, ladies. We are going to change the game. To Side Chicks Unite." We huddled and did a group hug and I could feel the love; it felt like one big happy family. Little did I know this feeling wouldn't last long and our family would become like any other dysfunctional family.

AUBREY

Side Chicks Unite had been in business for six months and I had received $125,000 of the church's money back. We finally rented all the apartments in the building. In all honesty we had more men interested in being sponsors than we had women available. I told Alexis that we needed to expand the operation, but she was so picky when it came to choosing the women. Although she put Autumn in charge of recruiting she still had the final say. I knew it would take some time to recoup the money and Alexis had been a doll about making sure that any extra money after expenses and paying Autumn went to paying the church back.

My business is still thriving and Alexis has become very popular due to her being on the radio; as a result she was in demand as a hostess and motivational speaker, so money wasn't an issue. Besides, money wasn't driving me or Alexis - we were driven by revenge.

I finally met Kia and she was the spitting image of Kai and KJ. I loved her immediately; I don't trust her mother - I think she is vying for my spot, but it will be a cold day in hell and the devil will wear ice skates before I just give him up. I will turn up if I have to, so if Kai wants to leave he will have to man up and leave. I will not make it easy for him. I have given up most of my side chicks and dudes. I needed to bring my sin count down since I borrowed the money from the church. I guess I need to pick a sin and just ride it out. I don't want to go to hell for stealing and adultery. When I walked into the church conference room for our meeting to plan the bishop's anniversary the first person I saw was Vanessa.

I hate to admit that I miss Vanessa. We were friends before we were lovers and I miss our friendship.

"Hello, first lady," everyone said in unison.

"Good afternoon, saints," I smirked. I know these heffas don't like me and they secretly want Kai. They can't have them either. As I was sitting down at the head of the conference table I receive a text from an unknown number: <u>would not God search this out? For He knows the secrets of the heart...</u> Before I could delete it I received another one. <u>The wages of sin are death...I advise you to repent, sinner.</u> Before I could add the number to the auto-reject list I received another one. <u>What's done in the dark will come to the light.</u> My hands started shaking. I could hear the women talking but I couldn't make out the words. I took a sip of water, inhaled and exhaled, and called the meeting to order.

AUTUMN

"MORGAN, LET'S GO! I AM tired of going through this with you every morning." I could hear her stomping down the stairs. "Don't make me slap the shit out of you this morning. Now stomp down my stairs one more time. Take your ass to bed at night and you won't have problems getting up in the morning. I promise you I will take every electronic item you own. Don't fuck with me." I swear if she rolled her eyes or neck I would have slapped her to sleep.

I was so tired this morning. I can't believe her daddy's grown rusty-ass wife had the nerve to call me at 4:00 am looking for her husband. I don't want his whorish ass and he's behind on his child support payments, so he damn sure can't come to my house and pull sheets. By the time I got to Morgan's bus stop the bus was driving off; instead of trying to flag the bus down I decided to drop her off at school. I looked over at her and she was putting on lip gloss. I started to slap her lips dry. While waiting for her to get out of the car I received a text messages from Alexis. <u>We need to meet, ASAP!</u>

ALEXIS

I STRUGGLED IN THE DARK to find my phone when I heard Shamika's text tone at 4:00 am. My stomach knotted up when I saw the picture of the positive pregnancy text with the caption "I got a bun in the oven" and a bunch of damn smiley face emojis. I sat straight up in the bed and hit call. She did not answer. I hate it when people send you a text and when you call them back they do not answer the damn phone. I knew she didn't want to talk to me, hence the damn text message. I swear verbal conversation is a lost art.

Oh, little Miss "I don't want no kids; I'm about getting my money" is going to have to face the music. I thought of all the women Shamika would be the smartest. She broke one of the rules of the organization and a pretty serious rule. I don't know how many times I stressed to the ladies to use birth control and to make him use a condom because if he is cheating on his wife they cannot be sure that wasn't seeing someone else. This is not going to turn out well.

I jumped out of bed and threw on my favorite black yoga pants, one of Autumn's old army PT shirts, and my white and black Polo flip-flops. I didn't bother to remove my multicolored yellow, gold, and orange silk scarf. My mission was getting to Shamika's apartment. I arrived at her apartment about 4:45 am. The only lights on were from the security apartment.

When I entered the building I was greeted by Jerome, the night security supervisor. I was surprised to see him standing at the door. I've heard rumors that he does the most while on duty. He's always late for work, but somehow convinces the other guys to cover for him until he gets there. There was even a rumor that he left the property on Wednesdays to go watch "Empire." I don't care as long as someone is on property; besides, Jerome is too old to be working security. Most of the people call him Grandpa.

I went into my office and attempted to call Shamika again. I know she was home because her blue BMW 325i was in her parking space. *This little bitch is trying it*, I thought. If she don't come to momma, then momma will come to her. I was glad Jerome was not in the hall when I walked up the stairs to Shamika's apartment. I rang the doorbell three times, but she did not answer so I used the master key and went in. "Shamika," I hollered. "Shamika! I know you are here; bring your ass out here right now!" She slinked her ass out of her bedroom wearing purple boy shorts and a matching tank top.

"What?!" she said while plopping down on her cream-colored sofa.

"What? What the fuck is this!?" I said, showing her the text she sent me.

"Oh, that," she replied. "I'm having Jason's baby and we are going to be a family."

"WTF...family? Little girl, he already has a family," I said through clenched teeth. "You broke the rules of this organization. I can't tell you to have an abortion - that is your choice to make, but Shamika, Jason is a powerful man who has his political career to worry about. Do you think that he is going to leave the woman who helped him get to where he is to be with his young side chick...baby mama?"

"Yes, he loves me. He told me he doesn't love her anymore. Besides, I can give him what she can't—a baby."

"You think a baby is going to keep a man?"

"This baby will, because he wants a son and he wants to be with me."

"Did he tell you that? Men lie and will tell you anything."

"He wants me! Why is it hard for you to believe that he could want me and want for us to be a family?"

"Because he wants his political career more and this affair with you and now the baby is suicide for his political career. You think his wife is just going to leave and let him live happily-ever-after? Honey, have you heard the saying 'hell hath no fury like a woman scorned?' Trust me, little girl, Marian is not going to let him go. She will hang on to him just to make him miserable."

"Well, I have no fucks to give to Marian. He will leave to be with me and his baby. Can you please leave? I am an expecting mother and I need to get my rest."

"No! I'll leave when I am good and Goddamn ready. I own this building." I lowered my voice and calmly said, "Listen, Shamika, I hope you really are pregnant. I know all about the false positive pregnancy test scams that young women like to use. This is not a game; you are messing with people's lives and feelings. This will not turn out well."

"Yes, I am pregnant!" she yelled while rolling her neck and turning up her lips. "This is going to turn out just fine...I always get what I want and I want to be the next Mrs. Carey," she said and walked back to her bedroom. I blocked her from closing the door and followed her in.

Leaning against the mahogany dresser I said, "Shamika, what happened to you wanting financial stability so you can start your own company? Are you going to throw away your dreams because of a man?"

"I'm not throwing away my dreams. I am going to support my man and we are going to raise our child."

"You are living in a fairy tale. Let me play the devil's advocate...say he does leave his wife. How secure are you going to feel in the relationship? I mean if he leaves Marian for you, then what makes you think he won't leave you for another woman?"

"'Cause I am woman enough to hold on to my man."

"You think Marian is not woman enough to hold on to her husband? His cheating has nothing to do with her or what she did or failed to do, but more to do with his character as a man. Think about it, little girl. He joined an organization that helped him cheat on his wife and he pays good money for it, too, he is taking money out of his family household. Do you think that won't happen to you?"

"Jason and I talked about that. He promised me that I was different and that we were meant to be together and that he would never cheat on me because I am the best thing that has ever happened to him."

"You have a lot to learn," I said, shaking my head. I wanted to grab her and try shake some sense into her. She doesn't have the sense God gave a cricket. "I guess your mind is made up."

"Yes, it is," she stated as a matter of fact.

"Well, you are still family and we love you, and we will be here for you and the baby," I replied.

As I was walking out the door she said, "I will be moving out of my apartment at the end of the month. Jason is getting me an apartment in Buckhead."

I stopped in my tracks. I looked at her and warned her not to leave. "Shamika, I don't think that is a good idea. Don't isolate yourself from your support group."

"Jason is all that I need. He said that the baby and I will be taken care of. I am going to yoga classes for pregnant women and all kinds of fun stuff. I'll meet some more pregnant women and they will be my support group."

"Do what you got to do," I said and walked out.

VANESSA

Aubrey was shaking like a leaf on a tree. The text messages had her shook. I bet she wished that Jesus would have stopped by and turned her water into wine. I made friends with Edith, the treasurer, so I could coach her into asking about the funds in the benevolence account. She was so slow and willing to kiss Aubrey's ass that she let Aubrey control the account, so she didn't know how much money was in the account.

When Aubrey excused herself to go to bathroom I sent another text: As you sow, so shall you reap. With whatever measure you mete out to others, with the same measures it shall be meted out to you. When she returned from the bathroom and read the text her face looked flushed. Her hands were shaking and her voice trembled when she said, "Now where were we?"

"Are you all right, baby?" Ms. Mary inquired.

"Yes, I just haven't been feeling well lately. I think I might be catching a cold or something," she replied. Catching a cold my ass. She'll wish that it was just a cold.

"Bishop Joseph is such a wonderful man of God and family man; I think we should have a weeklong celebration. We can have activities at the church all week; on Saturday we can have family day and climax all the events on Sunday with one service and just go all out to celebrate this wonderful man of God and his family," I suggested. All the women loved the idea.

"How are we going to pay for it?" Edith asked. "I don't think we should collect money from the congregation; I think this should be a gift to them from the church," I said. Aubrey looked at me suspiciously but didn't say anything. I smiled and looked away.

"We need to establish a budget so we will know if we have enough money in the church miscellaneous fund," Aubrey said.

"I will check the funds," Edith said. I gave her a blank stare. I told this bitch to have the information ready for this meeting. *If you want something done you have to do it yourself.* Smiling, I said, "Edith, if you need help, please let me know. I want this to be a great week for the bishop, his wife, and the church."

"We can work on it after the meeting," Edith replied nervously. I know she is such an Aubrey-pleaser and she didn't want to make any waves. I just kept fueling the fire. I looked at Aubrey and asked, "First lady would you like to help us go over the funds and establish the budget."

"I will leave it up to the two of you. My schedule is busy this week. After you set a budget, then we can get together and finalize everything. Next week we can meet and assign people to the various areas they will be responsible for, and in the meantime we need to get as many volunteers as possible," Aubrey said.

"I will create a PowerPoint and give it to the media ministry, so they can put it on the church website and show it during both services on Sunday," I said.

"That's a wonderful idea. Thank you, Vanessa, for all your help," Aubrey responded.

"No problem," I replied. We agreed to meet the following Monday. When Aubrey rose from her seat my heart ached and longed for her. I missed her deeply and I loved her more than I could love any man or woman. I was torn between getting revenge for her ending our relationship and just letting her live her life. I knew that Aubrey was torn between her sexuality and living her life to please others. If she would have the heart that her oldest sister had this wouldn't be an issue. Alexis lived her life on her terms and didn't give a damn what other people thought.

Aubrey and I made eye contact and I could tell she missed me. She hurt my feelings when she walked past me like I was invisible. This pissed me off and made me more determined to make her sure I wasn't the only one with hurt feelings. I sent another text: <u>Thou shall not commit adultery.</u>

JASON

I CAN'T BELIEVE SHAMIKA TEXTED me a picture of a positive pregnancy test. If she is really pregnant I don't know what I am going to do. I've been through this before four years ago when Debra Wilson said she was pregnant and it turned out to be fake. She was tricky; she took two negative pregnancy tests, opened them and put them together so they would look positive. She even told Marian that she was pregnant. Marian didn't believe her and forced her to take a pregnancy test in our bathroom. It was negative. Marian has been trying to get pregnant again, since she had a miscarriage three years ago. I tried to get her to adopt, but she was adamant that she was going to have a baby. If she finds out about this she will be devastated and angry. I don't know how she will react this time; I promised her that it would never happen again.

An affair that produces an outside child is suicide to my political career. This could not have come at a worse time. I've been asked to be the running mate for Democratic presidential candidate Hunter Mills. The Republican Party would have a field day. This would hand them the White House. They are dying to get a Republican president back in the White House, especially after having a Democrat and African-American President in there for two terms.

I love Mika, but I am not sure if leaving Marian is a good idea. Mika is not as refined as Marian and she doesn't have her money or connections. Marian comes from a family of old money. She grew up in Waterbury, Connecticut. She can be a little judgmental and snooty and she has a temper from hell. When she gets mad she is like the Tasmanian devil. I'm not sure how she will react if she finds out that her money is helping take care of Mika. Damn what have I done.

SHAMIKA

ALEXIS' LITTLE VISIT LAST NIGHT didn't trouble my spirit none. I knew she was looking out for me and wanted what was best for me. I know that I broke some of the cardinal rules of SC Unite, but I don't care. I am in love with a man who loves me and who is going to take care of me and our child. I will have the life that I didn't have growing up and my child will be born with a silver spoon in his or her mouth.

Jason was not happy when I texted him a picture of the pregnancy test. He and Alexis said the same thing about women texting men fake positive pregnancy tests. I was surprised at their ages; they were up on game. Jason made me take another pregnancy test in front of him. The results were positive. He didn't ask me to have an abortion. He told me he was moving me to another apartment and that he would make sure that we were taken care of and not to worry about a thing. I feel sorry for women like Alexis who have been tricked by married men who never left their wives for them.

Well, I am not one of them. I know how to get and keep a man. Maybe I will put them up on game like I did with Sia. She was here when I took the first pregnancy test. I sent her the same picture I sent to Jason and Alexis and told her to use it to get her man. Her sponsor is a powerful music mogul who is married to a loud ratchet chick. She lacks the class and sophistication that we have learned at SC Unite. Sia is a little too naïve, though; when I told her to text the pregnancy test she started asking too many questions, like what if he wants me to take another? How will I explain when the dates don't add up? What if I can't get pregnant soon?

I had to break everything down to her. First of all, if he makes you take another, then just say the first test was faulty and act relieved like you didn't want to be pregnant in the first place. If he doesn't ask for a pregnancy test and you have problems getting pregnant, wait until he is out of town and then tell him you had a miscarriage. If you get pregnant don't worry about the dates; the DNA will confirm that he is the father. I have a feeling that Sia's sponsor is not going to feel the same way. He loves his loud-ass ratchet wife. It's worth a try. If he moves her out of SC Village, then the money he is paying Alexis can go in her pocket along with what she is already receiving. I hope she gets pregnant so we can go to the yoga classes for expecting mothers together. Maybe she could move into the same condos as me in Buckhead and our kids could play together. This was going to be great. Thank you, SC Unite, for the come-up and far as the slogan, "We didn't say I do, so fuck you," I have a new slogan: "Sorry I broke the rules, but I got to do what I got to do!"

ALEXIS

A HARD HEAD MAKES A soft ass. Growing up I heard my grandmother say that phrase over and over. Shamika was playing with fire and was about to get burned. She's so damn smart she is stupid. That little girl had a lot to learn about life and she was in for a bumpy ride. I was fuming after I left her apartment. I went to Walmart and walked around the store for no apparent reason. The third shift workers were everywhere, stocking shelves, waxing the floors, trying to navigate around shoppers like myself who were not really buying anything - just in the way. My heart empathized with the third shift workers. I understood the struggle and admired their tenacity to work overnight to earn money. I worked third shift and by 4:00 am the struggle was real. There were many times I wanted to find a dark secluded corner and curl up in the fetal position and just sleep until times got better. One thing I know - when you come off third shift it takes a long time for your body to bounce back.

I couldn't quiet my mind. I couldn't help but think about the situation brewing at SC Unite. It made me wonder how many other women would not follow the rules and would get pregnant on purpose in an attempt to trap their sponsor. I wondered what's going through Jason's mind and how much of what Shamika said was true. I know this man wanted to eventual reside at 1600 Pennsylvania Avenue; he couldn't possibly be thinking about leaving Marian for Shamika. We trained her well at SC Unite. She was refined thanks to our finishing training; she was educated and has the ability to handle herself in social situations, but she is no match for Marian Carey.

This scandal will not be good...no good can come out of Jason getting Shamika pregnant, especially after all the trials and tribulations he and Marian have had trying to have a baby. I couldn't help but wonder if this will endanger the secrecy of SC Unite. I have other clients to think about and since Shamika has gone rogue I doubt if she will abide by the non-disclosure form that she signed.

I was torn - on one hand, I wanted revenge against men because I was hurt by a few and hurt people hurt people, but on the other hand I don't want Marian to be hurt. This sounded like a good idea at the time - now it is a bad idea gone wrong. I felt like a hypocrite. I was so hurt when Michael cheated on me, I wanted his head on a platter. I wanted him to hurt like I was hurting, but then I turned around and helped men cheat for financial gain. I got to keep the organization together; at least, until I get Aubrey's investment back to the church.

I sat in my Lexus in the Walmart parking lot and texted Aubrey and Autumn. It was six o'clock in the morning and I knew they both would be up. Autumn would be getting Morgan ready for school and getting ready for work, and Aubrey would be up with KJ. I swear that little boy gets up with the roosters. I kept his little ass twice; he can't spend the night with me anymore until he gets grown. It made me rethink wanting to have kids - he was in everything. I couldn't go to the bathroom by myself. I sent Bre and Autumn a group text: We need to meet, ASAP! I pulled out of the Walmart parking lot and headed back towards SC Unite.

* * *

My eyes were bloodshot from the lack of sleep. As usual Autumn was the first to arrive. "What is going on?" Autumn asked.

"We have situation. I will tell you everything when Aubrey gets here. I don't want to keep repeating the story."

"You know she is always the last one to arrive. Spill the tea; I can't stand the suspense. You know my nerves are bad." I looked at Autumn and she looked tired, too. I ignored her by asking, "Why do you look so tired?"

"Girl, my baby daddy's wife called me at four o'clock asking me if I had seen her husband."

"Girl, stop!"

"I'm serious. I was mad as hell."

"What did you say, Autumn?"

"I told that wench 'I don't know where your husband is; hell he wasn't with me.' I had a moment of weakness, but I don't want a man I got to hit in the head with a weed whacker," she laughed. I shook my head and put it down on the desk. "You look like hell, Lexi. What in the hell is going on and why you got on your fighting clothes?" Autumn said.

"Child, these are not fighting clothes. I am too old and too grown to be fighting."

"Whatever; you look a mess, so what's going on that I have to be late for work to come here?"

"Please, you are late for work every day."

"That's not the issue. I like to be late on my own. I don't need people to help me be late," she smirked.

Laughing, I said, "You are a mess. I can't with you this morning."

Finally, Aubrey walked in looking like she had come straight off the runway. Her hair was parted down the middle and put up in a ponytail. Her makeup was flawless; she was wearing a red pencil skirt and a houndstooth off-the-shoulder silk blouse and a pair of black red bottoms. I looked her up and down and rolled my eyes. "Where are you going, diva?" I asked.

She slid behind her desk and patted the bun in her head and said, "Nowhere. I just like to look my best." Autumn got up and walked to the mini refrigerator, got a bottle of apple juice, and said, "Now that the fashion queen is here, can you tell us why we are here? I need to get to work."

"Girl, please. You don't give a rat's ass about going to work," Aubrey said.

"Right," I chimed in. "Now sit down and drink your juice," I added.

"Damn, Lex, you look like hell," Aubrey said.

"Thank you for that observation. I do what I can do when I can do it," I joked. I took a deep breath and told them about Shamika getting pregnant and our conversation. They looked worried as I recounted the events of my early morning confrontation with Shamika. I showed them the text message with the picture of the pregnancy test. "How do we know this is not a fake test or someone else's test?" Aubrey inquired.

"We don't. If it is a lie she is riding with it and she has Jason convinced because she is moving out of her apartment at the end of the month," I replied.

"Well, damn, I thought she was smart. I guess we met her representation," Autumn said.

"I knew something was not quite right with that girl the moment I saw her with the Ross, Marshall, and TJ Maxx designer clothes and handbag. She was trying too hard," Aubrey added.

"How do you know her clothes came from Ross and Marshall?" Autumn asked.

"I used to work in the fashion industry...duh," Aubrey quipped.

"Thelma and Louise, can we focus? We got to get some legs on this situation or at least have a plan for damage control. Shamika is in love and is not thinking logically, so it is just a matter of time before Marian Carey finds out. Once she does the shit is going to hit the fan. Besides, we've got to protect the identity of the rest of the sponsors and girls. If there is fallout from this I will protect both of your identities. I will be the face of SC Unite and neither one of you knew anything about this," I said.

Aubrey shook her head no and said, "Alexis, we are in this together... family is all we got," then she started singing, "We ride together we die together...bad girls, bad girls, what you going to do?"

I interrupted her and said, "You have KJ and Autumn has Morgan. I can't jeopardize you both being away from your babies. This was my bright idea. If the media gets a hold of this we will probably be viewed as a brothel and it will be said that I was running a prostitution ring." I watched Aubrey as she strutted to the window. She turned around and kicked off her red bottoms.

"Okay, so here is what we need to do. First, Lexi, remove the external hard drive from the safe deposit box. Don't close it; we will put some expensive jewelry in it. I will hide the external drive at the safe in the church," Aubrey explained.

"Church?" Autumn and I said in unison.

"Yes, if there is an investigation the police will go through everything you own, so we have to move the evidence. We have a few safes at the church and I have my own personal safe and can you think of anywhere safer than the Lord's house?" I looked at my sister with so much love. She was really going out on a limb for me. I was determined to protect them both and she was trying to protect me.

I was going to meet with Mr. Jason Carey to find out where his head is and what the hell he had been telling that little girl. Yes, Jason and I would have a come-to-Jesus meeting soon.

JASON

I KNEW ALEXIS WOULD CALL when Shamika told me about their impromptu meeting in the middle of the night. I want a baby and Shamika is fine, and she and I could have a good marriage, but I have worked so hard to get where I am and this could ruin my career. I wish Alexis would have agreed to be my girlfriend. I wouldn't be going through this right now.

I should have picked another woman out of the bunch, but I was mesmerized by Shamika's youthfulness and tight body. I should have never trusted a big butt and a smile. This situation would be so much easier if I was single. I feel like Richard Dimples Fields in his song "She Got Papers." I used to love Marian so much; she held me down when I was in law school. She has done so much for me and even went against her family to be with me when they didn't approve of me. If they find out about this her mom will say 'I told you so.' They looked down on me because I was from a small town in Alabama; I heard her mother call me Bama a few times. I am not embarrassed about my roots. I appreciate where I came from; I am a true southern gentleman.

Marian's and my relationship is over. I feel sorry for her even though she acts confident deep down inside she has insecurities. Losing the babies and having problems getting pregnant has taken its toll on her and how she views herself as a woman. She feels like if she can't bring a child into the world that makes her less of a woman. I told her many times that we could adopt; there are a lot of African-American kids that need a loving home. We could have provided that and so much more. Marian was so stubborn, she would not even consider adoption.

Alexis agreed to meet me at 8:00 pm at my loft in downtown Atlanta. Marian and I bought the loft when we first moved to Atlanta. We used it as rental property income; however, the tenants moved out three months ago and I decided not to rent it and use it as a place where I could go for some 'me' time. The solitude of the loft gives me a chance to reflect and recharge from the stresses of my job and wife. I considered moving Shamika into it, but Marian knows the tenants moved out and I decided not to rent it, so it was too close for comfort.

When I arrived at my loft I took a long shower. I poured some Midnight for Men body wash onto exfoliation gloves and rubbed it all over my body. I stood in the shower and let the hot water run all over my body while I meditated. When I stepped out of the shower I wiped the steam off the mirror and rubbed coconut oil over my wet skin before drying off with a bath towel. I then rubbed Midnight for Men lotion all over my skin and put on a pair of black Calvin Klein boxer briefs and a black ribbed tank shirt. My face was starting to get a five o'clock shadow, so I decided to shave. I rubbed some Luster S-curl lite wave gel activator on my hair. I don't know why I was going through this extra grooming: Alexis meeting me was not a date. I didn't want to seem like I was trying too hard, so I dressed casual: I put on a pair of Tom Ford black trousers, a Salvatore Ferragamo Bengal black and white striped button-down shirt, and a pair of black Tom Ford oxfords. I took a bottle of Pinot Grigio out of the wine freezer and put it on ice. I made a fruit and cheese tray with crackers just in case Alexis wanted a light snack. I turned on the TV and watched "Family Feud" while I waited.

Alexis arrived twenty minutes early for our meeting. I had to meet her at the gate to let her into the courtyard for my building. "I hope you don't mind me arriving early," she said smiling as we entered my loft.

"No, not at all," I replied, leading her downstairs to the living room. "Please have a seat," I said.

My little head was thinking she could definitely get it. She was dressed casually fine. She wore a high-waisted black skirt with a side split and a black and white polka-dot blouse and red pumps. Her hair was pulled back into a ponytail. She wasn't wearing lot of make-up; her hazel eyes sparkled. *Damn, I wish she was on the SC Unite menu.* She looked so classy. She didn't walk through the door - she strutted with so much confidence and when she sat down and crossed her legs I could see part of her silky smooth thigh. "I hate being late and I hate wasting people's time. I feel that time is something that you cannot get back," she explained

"I understand. My dad used to say if you are on time you are late. He was in the military and always had to be in formation fifteen minutes early," I said, sitting on the corner of the sofa closest to where she was sitting.

"This is a very nice place you have."

"Thank you. It was my rental property, but when the tenants move out I decided to keep it as my private little hideaway."

"Oh," she smirked.

"What?" I asked, acting coy.

"Nothing, no judgment. I guess everyone needs a space they can call their own. Most men just get a man cave; you got a whole loft," she laughed.

"So, you got jokes?" I laughed.

"Nope...just call it as I see it."

"Would you like something to drink?" I asked. I got up from the sofa and walked up the stairs to the kitchen

"Sure...what do you have?" She sashayed up the stairs to the kitchen as I said, "I have water, soda, and wine." I was hoping she would choose wine. I wanted her to relax, especially considering the cause for our meeting.

"I need something stronger than water or soda. My nerves are bad, so I'll have a glass of wine," she said. I popped the cork on the Pinot Grigio and poured her a glass and a glass for myself. I handed her the wine.

"Thank you."

"You are welcome." Sipping on her wine she asked, "Do you have any snacks?"

I smiled and took the fruit, cheese, and cracker trays out of the refrigerator. She turned up her nose and said, "You don't have any meat to go with those cheese and crackers?"

"Are you hungry?"

"Yes, I haven't eaten today."

"Well, let me order something...I mean, if you are not in a rush. That is the least I can do."

"Thank you...that is mighty white of you," she joked. I liked that she had a sense of humor. Beauty, brains, and funny - she was my kind of woman.

"Do you like pizza?" I asked.

Her eyes lit up. "I love pizza! I could eat it every day," she exclaimed.

"Great, I know this little mom-and-pop place. Their pizza is the bomb," I said. After we decide on the toppings I placed an order for pizza and lemon pepper hot wings. While we waited for the food I decided it was time to talk about the elephant in the room. Looking into her hazel eyes I whispered, "So, I guess we need to discuss the reason for the meeting." Pouring another glass of wine and putting a grape in her mouth Alexis nodded her head in agreement. Slowly she said, "What are you telling Shamika?"

"What do you mean?"

"Did you tell her that you love her and that you are going to leave Marian to be with her?" she asked.

"Not in so many words."

Alexis gave me the 'nigga please' look and said, "Then what words did you use? That little girl is in love with you and she thinks she is the cat's meow and that you are going to divorce your wife, so you, her, and the baby can live happily-ever-after."

"I'll admit I told her more about my situation with Marian than I should have. I'll admit that I do love her. I can't force her to have an abortion, so I will take care of my child. I might have said that I would leave Marian."

"Do you love her?"

"Yes, I do."

"Did you want her to have your baby?"

"If I wasn't married I would be happy for her to have my baby. A man wants to leave a seed...a legacy. But an outside child could hurt my political career. I don't know how my wife is going to act. I honestly don't want to be married to her anymore, but I am not sure if Shamika is the woman for me. I mean, she is a beautiful young woman and she is fun, but she wants to live the baller life. She watches a lot of reality shows and idolizes those women. I think she is better suited for a basketball player or musician."

"Why didn't you use a condom every time you had sex with her? You didn't think about protecting your wife. I mean, we have the women tested for sexually transmitted diseases, but we are not with them all day every day and we don't know what goes on behind closed doors. Also, we have them sign contracts, but that doesn't mean they will honor those contracts. You see how this turned out. Shamika broke so many rules of the organization it makes my head spin."

I was speechless. I could tell that Alexis was vexed by this situation. "You are absolutely right. I should have used a condom each and every time."

"You damn right I am right. You and Shamika have put this organization and the other members at risk. I can't trust Shamika to keep quiet about who her baby daddy is and you moved her out of the village. So you are encouraging her to go rogue."

"Moved her out of the building? She told me you kicked her out!"

"I didn't kick her out. I damn near begged her to stay so that she would have us for support. She pretty much gave me her ass to kiss. She said you were moving her out so you two could be a family." Shaking her head she took another sip of wine.

"Well I'll be damn," I said.

"A lie don't care who tell it," Alexis responded.

Suddenly my cellphone rang. "That must be our food," I said, walking towards the door. I went outside and paid for the food. When I returned to the loft I put the pizza on the kitchen counter. Alexis sat down on the brown counter-height bar stool and watched me while I put the food on the plate. "If you like, we can eat in the living room," I suggested. She followed me back to the living room. We both sat down on the sofa and I handed her the plate of food.

"Thank you," she said.

"You are welcome." We ate in silence. I loved watching her eat. I noticed that she never put the chicken bone up to her mouth she always pulled the meat off the bone. She saw me looking and said, "What?" I laughed and said, "You eating that chicken all cute. In the south we suck the meat off the bone." I licked my lips and thought I wish she was this chicken. I knew we needed to finish talking about Shamika, so I started the conversation again. "Alexis, I am sorry that I have put you and your and organization in the middle of my mess. I will handle it...trust me. I promise."

"Trust you? I have my own plan in place for damage control because it's not just about me. It's about my sisters, the other women, and men."

"You can trust me. I got you."

I decided to take a chance and hit on her again. I looked into her mesmerizing hazel eyes and said, "If you would have been my girlfriend, we would not be having this discussion. We would be making love right now." She bit her bottom lip and turned her head. I could tell she was blushing.

"I explained to you that I gave up Side Chickism."

"Too bad for me," I pouted.

"Really? Pouting? It's not a good look."

"You can't fault a brother for trying."

"I'll give you an 'A' for effort." We put our plates down at the same time." I picked up her wine glass and handed it to her, then picked up mine and said, "Let's toast."

"To what?"

"To a good friendship."

"Cheers," she said and we clanked glasses. I put our wine glasses on the table and moved in for a kiss. To my surprise she didn't resist.

SHAMIKA

I TEXTED JASON TWENTY TIMES last night and he didn't text back. When I called his personal cell phone my call went straight to voice mail. I called his work phone because he's supposed to have it on at all times and it just rang. This was so unlike Jason not to respond to my text or calls. He would find a way to call me back even if it meant he had to talk to me from his garage. I bet that bitch was acting thirsty, hanging onto my man like luggage.

I'll be so happy when he leaves and moves in with me and our child. I know I lied to him about Alexis telling me that I had to move out, but I wanted to see if he really loved me and would take care of me outside of the organization. So far I have not wanted for anything, but time. It is hard being pregnant by a married man. He couldn't go with me to the doctor, so Sia went with me for my first ultrasound. I love my girl to the moon and back; however, I would have liked for my baby daddy and future husband to be there holding my hand and seeing our little peanut on the monitor for the first time.

I hope Jason doesn't drag this divorce thing out because I am going to need his physical presence as well as emotional support, and he is going to have to go to the store for me when I start having crazy cravings. I definitely don't want to have this baby by myself. I have thought about helping his divorce along by calling that thing he is married to and telling her that I am expecting his child.

I was so frustrated with Jason that I was restless and I woke up tired. I texted him Good morning handsome, I hope everything is all right. I love you! J After an hour he still didn't respond, so I called his personal phone and it still went to voicemail. My stomach felt nervous and my heart was pounding. I hung up and called his work phone and it just rang and rang and then I heard, "Your call has been forwarded to an automated voice mail system. (404)391-9111 is not available. At the tone, please record your message. When you are finished you may hang up or please press one for more options. Beep." I was so confused. It was not like Jason to not call or text me back. I hadn't heard from him since yesterday morning after I texted him a picture of the baby's first ultrasound. I know he has a lot on his mind with his career and wanting to eventually become President of the United States. I know having a baby out of wedlock is frowned upon and people will judge him for cheating on his wife. But, we are in love.

I was so nervous I didn't have an appetite. I paced back and forth from the bedroom to the kitchen. I wanted to cry, but the tears would not flow. I knew something was not right. I could feel it in my spirit. I prayed that my honey was all right and that he would call me soon. I was starting to get mad at myself for falling in love with a married man and getting pregnant on purpose. I just knew that he would want to be with me and the baby. I just knew it. I felt so much discord that I called my bestie to help me calm my nerves. I've been schooling Sia on getting Malik Jackson to leave that big-head heffa he is with and marry her. This dude is a music mogul and is loaded with money, power, and fame. Sia needs to be on his arms at all the music award shows and red carpet events. She is much prettier than China Jackson and thanks to SC Unite more refined. One thing I can say about the organization is they set you up for success. I feel kind of bad about not following the rules...it is what it is. I got to get me, me. When Sia answered the phone I could I could hear a hint of sadness in her voice.

"Hey, girl," I sighed. Sia was quiet so I said, "What's wrong, Si?"

"Girl, everything," she sobbed. She was crying so hard I forgot about my feelings and tried to calm her down. "Sia, calm down so I can understand what you are saying. What's wrong?"

"I did like you said and I texted Malik a copy of the pregnancy test. He came over and brought me money to get an abortion and told me that he would arrange for me to have a ride to the clinic. When I told him that I didn't want an abortion, that I wanted to have his child and I wanted us to be a family, he went off. He grabbed me by my neck and said that I better have an abortion or he is going to stomp the baby out of me. Mika, I have never seen him this mad. It was like I didn't even know him. He called me a stupid bitch and said that he loved his wife and he would never leave her for a high-priced whore."

"What?! I am so sorry, Sia. I just thought that it worked for me and Jason and that it could work for you."

"Well, it didn't, and now he doesn't want to be with me anymore. What am I going to do? I can't lose him...I love him. I messed up. I just want him back." Sia sounded so desperate I didn't know what to say. I had given her the wrong advice. I guess not all men are like my boo. Sia was crying so hard I didn't want to end the conversation, but when I looked at the clock on the microwave it was 10:16 am, I needed to get ready for my first yoga class for expectant mothers. So I said, "Get dressed and go with me to yoga class and after class we will figure this out."

She stopped crying and responded, "Yoga? Are you talking about for pregnant women?"

"Yes, now get dressed. I'm picking you up in forty-five minutes."

"Ok." I hung up with Sia and texted Jason again.

AUBREY

Every time I block these random numbers that I've received text messages from, I receive another one from a different number. This morning while feeding KJ some scrambled eggs, sausage links, and pancakes. I received: Hell hath no fury like a woman scorned ☹. My hands shook so bad that I dropped the food off the spoon before it made it to my baby's mouth. KJ looked at me, laughed, picked the food up off his high chair tray, and stuffed it in his mouth and then he started trying to feed me. I pretended to eat the food. I love my child, but I am not eating after him; he has saliva on everything.

I have to get the remaining $175,000 of the church's money back quickly. Edith called me the other day asking to see the balance for the benevolence account. Edith is mousy and scared of her own shadow. She is a fashion misfit who thinks that to be saved she has to wear old-maid clothes. I get so tired of her signature long elastic-waist skirts and cardigan ensembles. She must have a cardigan in every color under the sun. Her Hush Puppy black shoes look like old nurse shoes. Her stringy long hair needs to be cut in a layered bob to give it some body. Many people call her black Olive Oyl behind her back.

I asked her why she needed this information and she said that she was trying to take a more active role in her treasurer duties. When she mentioned that she needed to get a clear picture on the finances so she could establish a budget for the bishop's anniversary, I shut her down. I explained to her that the benevolence fund is to help church members and not for church activities and that we could not borrow or commingle money. I told her I would email her a copy of the bank statement for the benevolence fund. I have yet to do it. Even with the drama with Shamicka Side Chicks Unite is making good money - we picked up some more sponsors and women.

I was determined to find out who is sending the text messages. I paid for a month's membership on Instant CheckMate so I could do a reverse number look-up. The numbers were cellphone carriers in Florida, California, and North Carolina. Due to my past indiscretions I have always been careful about what I do on the computer that Kai and I share and my laptop. I am a little paranoid, so I have both checked for spyware monthly just to make sure that Kai is not trying to track me. I don't worry about my Surface Pro 3; it is used strictly for business.

AUTUMN

I DECIDED TO HANG OUT at the office after work while I waited for Morgan to finish basketball practice. As soon as I pulled into the parking lot I was surprised to see Jerome, the night security manager for the property, on the golf cart. *He's here early he must be working a double shift.* I guess the security company will hire anybody, since they are not required to carry a gun. I can tell that back in the day he was fine. When he first started his hair was salt and pepper and he really looked distinguished, but he dyed his hair black and when he sweats the color runs down the side of his face and neck. He talks so loud even when he tries to whisper. And he loves to gossip. I must say when he is here he sees everything with them thick-ass round glasses with grey electrical tape on the rim. As I was taking my tote bag out of the car Jerome drove over and started talking. "You need some help with that, Ms. Autumn?" he asked, while staring at my breast.

"Oh, no, thank you Jerome, I got it!" I looked up and I saw Malik coming out of the building at a fast pace. I could tell by the look on his face he was 38 hot. He peeled out of the parking.

"It's a shame these young men ain't got no manners. I know he saw us standing here," Jerome said.

"It looks like he has a lot on his mind," I responded.

"Yeah, well, I guess he do," Jerome said, looking down the top of his glasses. "I wonder who he is? He kind of look like that rapper Malik. I can't see that well because I got gatarats."

"You got what?" I asked.

"Gatarats - you know, I can't see well; that's why I wear glasses."

"Oh, you have cataracts."

"Well, that's what I said...Old Rome can't see like he used to." I couldn't help but smile. This man knows he will mispronounce words.

Trying to get a pulse of what's been happening on the property, I continued the small talk. "So how have you been doing? The last time I talked to you, you were having some medical problems. Are you doing better?" I inquired. I knew that getting him to talk about his health conditions would lead to him telling everything he has seen. Jerome took the bait; he leaned back in the seat on the golf cart and started talking. "Well, you know I got the sugar," he said.

"Yes, you told me before you had diabetes."

"Well, now I got to give myself shots. That's why sometimes I get weak...my hands be shaking like a leaf on a tree and I have to leave and go get something because my sugar be acting up, but I make sure that somebody is here to replace me. Can't nobody say that Jerome leave this property unsecured." I looked at him with so much empathy. He doesn't know that many of the people he works with have thrown him under the bus. The only reason he still has a job is because Alexis has a soft spot in her heart for him because he is originally from Detroit and she said they don't pay him enough to do right. As long as someone is here, especially at night, then she doesn't care. She is getting a TV put in their office so they can watch TV and maybe he will stop leaving to go watch his shows.

"I understand if you have to leave for medical reasons. As long as you have someone to cover for you it's all good."

"Well, I make sure somebody is here at all times. I like you and your sisters...y'all are nice to me."

"Thank you, we like you, too. Besides, Southwest Detroit got to stick together," I said.

"I know that's right," he laughed and then exited the golf car. I can tell he was ready to gossip.

"Well, let me get inside the office and see what is going on," I said.

"Well, I'll walk with you. Make sure you get in there all right."

"Thank you, that is so nice of you."

"I heard that girl Mika moved out."

"Yes, Shamika did move out." I looked at him side eye. I could tell he wanted to say more.

"Well, she came by here today and picked up her friend girl," he whispered.

"Who? Sia?"

"Yes, I can't pronounce her name I just call her Si. I don't know why our people have to give their kids such fancy names. What happened to plain names like Mary or Kay?" he laughed. Laughing and shaking my head I stuck the key in the door and I said, "I don't know. It is just a mess." Jerome held the door open for me, so I invited him in so I could pick him for more information.

"Come on in," I offered. Jerome walked in, shut the door, and stood still. "Please have a seat," I said. I turned on the TV and put my bag on my desk. "So Mika was here today?" I asked.

"Yes, she didn't come in the building though. She was sitting in the parking lot on her phone and then Si came out and got in the car with her and they drove off."

"Did she come back yet?"

"Yes, she brought her back about thirty minutes before that young man that look like the rapper Malik came. I seen him twice today. You know they say everybody got a twin and his twin was sure here today." I remained silent and looked at Jerome and from the look in his eyes I knew he knew that was rap mogul Malik, but he wanted me to confirm his suspicions.

"Would you like something to drink? We have some peach tea, water, and orange juice."

"I will have some tea, thank you." I opened the refrigerator and handed him a bottle of peach tea. I waited for him to take a drink and then started asking him questions.

"So, that guy that looks like the rapper - have you seen him here before?"

"I sure have. He has been here many nights. He don't stay all night... just two or three hours."

"Really?"

"Yes, like I said he's been here twice... this morning and this afternoon. When he left Mika showed up about thirty minutes later. Si looked like she had been crying. I ain't one to gossip, but I heard some loud talking coming from her apartment when he was here the first time."

"This morning? How long have you been here?" I asked.

"I came at seven o'clock this morning. I was a little late because the traffic on 85. They needed someone to fill in and well old Rome got to get his money."

"I ain't mad at you. Get your money. So you said you heard loud talking? Did it sound like they were arguing?"

"Yes, it made me nervous...my shingles came out... see?" he said while raising his shirt.

"No, no, put that back down," I said.

"Oh, but I didn't hear no furniture moving or nothing like that, just loud talking," he responded while tucking his shirt back in his pants.

"I hope Sia is all right. Please keep an eye on things for me and if you hear or see anything out of the ordinary, please call the police and call me or Alexis immediately."

"I sure will," Jerome said while getting up from his chair. "I better get out of here and patrol the property. I don't want heard told that Jerome slacked on the job."

I laughed and said, "Ok, Jerome. It was nice talking to you." I walked Jerome to the door, locked it, and called Alexis.

ALEXIS

IT WAS NINE O'CLOCK IN the morning when I woke up. I couldn't believe that I had sex with Jason. I think I did it out of spite - to prove that a man is going to be a man. I also wanted to show him that his young baby momma or prude wife can't hold a candle to a mature open-minded woman. I could blame it on the wine, but I have never needed alcohol to do what I wanted to do.

I liked Jason's loft all tucked away in downtown Atlanta in the old fourth ward. It used to be an old mattress factory. His place was small and cozy; it was a mixture of concrete, brick, and pipes. When he led me to the living room we walked past the contemporary kitchen with stainless-steel appliances. I had to walk down a wrought-iron staircase with unpainted concrete stairs to get to the living room. There was a fifty-five-inch flat-screen TV on the only wall that was not brick. The furnishings were earth tones: he had a tan sofa and loveseat with rust, brown, and tan pillows thrown on them; a brown leather chair sat in the corner next to a wall that had glass shelves with statues of Buddha on them. There was a glass and wrought-iron coffee table with some books and chess set on it. African and abstract art was placed all around the room. There was a painting easel and photography equipment next to his glass and wrought-iron saw-stand desk.

I learned that all the paintings on the walls were his. Painting was his passion, but since he entered the political arena it was now his hobby. The loft was the only place he could paint. He explained that Marian didn't mind him using the loft to paint and for photography because she didn't want his paint and other tools in the house. According to him, she felt that it was a waste of time and that his focus should be on getting to the White House one day and being the Vice-President would set him up to be the next President.

He told me he would rather paint than deal with all the evils of politics. When he graduated from law school his goal was to be a civil rights lawyer, but Marian encouraged him to go into corporate law. Painting helped him to escape from that world and when he was painting or taking pictures of landscapes he was the happiest. He wanted to have an art show to showcase his paintings, but Marian was against it. At one point he thought about leaving politics and retiring to a Caribbean island.

Being with Jason was comfortable; he was handsome, smart, a gentleman, and had a great sense of humor. When he kissed me I didn't resist. I could taste the wine on his tongue as we French kissed. I leaned back and crossed my legs so the split in my skirt would reveal more skin. Jason looked at me, licked his lips, and started rubbing my right thigh. He kissed me once again while moving his other hand up my shirt and unhooking the front snap on my bra. He planted kisses down my neck and I felt like I was going to explode. I wanted this man so bad. He stopped kissing me and took my hand and led me upstairs past the kitchen to his bedroom. "Have a seat," he said in a low husky voice. I sat on the bed and watched him turn on his Samsung Galaxy Tab and put on Teddy Pendergrass Radio on Samsung Milk Music app. He walked back to me and took off my shirt and started kissing me again. Our lips locked for what seemed like eternity. I unbuckled his pants; he looked sexy in his Calvin Klein boxer briefs and I could tell that he was working with something. I laid back on the bed. "Relax and be still. Tonight is all about you," he said. I closed my eyes and relished the moment "Are you all right?" he smirked.

"Yes," I whispered. I opened my eyes and watched his chocolate body as he walked to the dresser and took out a box of condoms. "Now you want to use a condom...where were your condoms when you was fucking Shamika?" I asked.

"I had them. I just didn't use them all the time."

"No," I said sarcastically. I got up and pushed him down on the bed and took the Magnum wrapper from him and opened it.

"Damn, you just going to take charge," he laughed.

"Honey, you ain't seen nothing yet," I said as I climbed on top of him and gave him the ride of his life.

VANESSA

EDITH IS SO SIMPLE; I finally manipulated her into challenging Aubrey about the bank statements. I arrived at church early so I could get in her ear. I didn't want her to see Aubrey and lose her confidence and not ask her about the money in front of all the women on the board. According to Edith, Aubrey was supposed to send her statement of all the accounts last week and still hadn't sent them. I don't know why this idiot didn't have access to the bank statements; after all, she was the damn treasurer of those accounts. Edith walked in looking like a thrown-away dishrag. No matter how hard she tried to fix herself up she missed the mark. "Hi, Edith," I greeted her with a smile and the usual church hug.

"Hi, Vanessa," she smiled.

"I am so glad you are here. I am really nervous about asking Aubrey about the bank statements in front of everyone."

"She still hasn't sent them?" I asked. "You know she is busy with the baby, her business, and being a wife. Aubrey wears a lot of hats, and then the poor thing is on a few committees at the church. I am sure it just slipped her mind," I explained.

"You know, you are probably right. I feel so bad adding something else to her plate, but like you said we need to know how much money we have so we can plan the activities for the bishop's anniversary."

"This is true. We do need to know how much money is available so we can finalize things and buy the necessary items we will need to make the events a success. Just ask her again in the meeting and maybe she can print them from the church's computer."

"That is a fantastic idea, Vanessa. I am so glad that you are on this committee. We are going to have so much fun working together," she squealed.

I smiled and said, "Yes, we are. I can't wait, Sister Edith. Let's wait for the rest of the women in the conference room." Little by little the rest of the committee arrived. I was surprised that Mrs. Divalicious, Aubrey, arrived on time.

"Ladies, thank you so much for coming today. I am excited that we are able to come together again for the planning of a week of wonderful events for the congregation and for the bishop," Aubrey said. She looked at me, I gave her a blank look. "Ms. Mary, would you lead us in prayer?" she said.

"Yes, I would!" Ms. Mary exclaimed and started praying. While Ms. Mary was praying I looked at Aubrey and thought *you are going to need more than prayers when I get finished with you, you selfish bitch.*

"Amen," everyone said in unison.

"Well, ladies, let's get down to business. Sister Edith, I know you and Sister Vanessa have been working on the budget and you need the bank statement for the miscellaneous account, so here it is," she said while handing her a copy of the bank statement. Edith took the statement and looked at it. "According to the statement we have $125,000. That should be more than enough for the bishop's anniversary celebration," Edith said.

"Yes, it should be. We have estimated that the total cost will be $75,000" I interjected. *Damn,* I thought to myself, she has skated out of this again. I scrambled, trying to figure out how to have Edith ask about the benevolence fund money. I knew that we couldn't legally transfer money from that account to the miscellaneous account. It seemed as if this bitch had divine intervention. Someone was definitely watching over her. I had to find out why she transferred that money to her personal account.

It brings me such joy to watch Aubrey squirm. She tried her best to maintain her composure, but her eyes gave it away. It made my heart sing to know that I had rattled her. It would take a little longer, but I would not be the only one hurting. *Maybe I am going about this wrong. I should try to repair our relationship in hopes that she will open up. She used to confide in me all the time.* In the meantime I will continue to send the text messages.

SHAMIKA

THE SOUND OF JASON'S RINGTONE woke me up. Finally! My baby is calling me...it's about time. I blew up both his phones with calls and text messages. "Hey baby, are you all right?" I asked.

"Yes, I'm good."

"Why haven't you been answering my calls? I called both numbers and sent you a gang of texts."

"I know, Mika, I just turned my personal phone back on and I just checked all the messages on my work phone."

"I was worried; you normally call or text me right back. I thought something was wrong and if something happened to you...how would I know? I mean I would have to hear about it on the news or on Facebook."

"Mika, I am fine. I just had some things I had to handle."

"Like what?"

"Well, first of all, I have to make sure that there is not any backlash from our situation."

"Backlash? Did you tell Marian?"

"No, not yet."

"Not yet? When are you going to tell her? I need you here with me and our baby. I can't...I will not go through this pregnancy alone, Jason. I am serious."

"What is that supposed to mean?"

"Nothing. I'm just letting you know I am not going through this pregnancy alone."

"You have to be patient. I can't just go home and tell her 'I'm leaving you for another woman who is having my baby.' Have you forgotten that I have been asked to run for Vice- President?"

"I don't give a fuck about that. You can do something that you've always wanted to do. You told me you really didn't care about politics."

"Things have to be done right and in order, Mika, and you will have to be patient, and that's all I have to say about that. Besides, we don't have to speak or see each other every day; it is not going to diminish our love."

I was steaming. I couldn't believe he was saying all this shit to me. I felt as if he was back-pedaling. My child will not be a secret. I will tear his world down. I sighed, "Do you still want to be with me and our child and be a family?"

"I don't know," he replied. My heart sanked. I started feeling anxious. "You don't know? What does that mean?" I asked.

"Just what I said...I don't know anymore. I never thought that a young boy who grew up poor in Enterprise, Alabama would have a chance to be the Vice-President of the United States of America."

Tears started streaming down my face. I maintained my composure I would not let him hear me cry. "What about me and our child?"

"The both of you will be well taken care of, I promise."

"So, let me get this straight. You will take care of us - you just don't want to be with us?"

"Mika, right now I am not sure. You lied to me and so now I don't know if I can trust you, I am taking things slow before I make my decision on whether I am going to leave Marian or stay."

"Lied? Lied to you about what!" I yelled.

"About getting kicked out your apartment. I didn't think anything about it at first since you broke the rules. If you lied about that it makes me wonder what else have you lied about."

I was fuming. He must have talked to that bitch Alexis. "Did you talk to Alexis?"

"As a matter of fact I did. She has to do damage control and she has to make sure the identities of the others in the organization are protected."

"Fuck her, fuck her organization, and fuck anyone else that thinks like her."

"That is such a childish and immature way of handling things. You knew what you were getting into when you joined, and it seems as if you changed music in the middle of the dance. It is not right, Mika. Please stop being selfish and think about someone other than yourself for a change."

"Fuck you!" I yelled and hung up the phone. I was so pissed. I immediately called Sia and her phone went to voicemail. What the fuck is going on...is this "don't answer Mika's calls" this week?

ALEXIS

When I arrived at SC Unite there were two police cars in the parking lot. "What is going on?" I asked Jerome.

"They showed up about an hour ago asking questions about Si."

"What kind of questions?" I asked. I couldn't put my finger on it, but my spirit felt uneasy.

"They wanted to know if she lived here and when was the last time anyone saw her."

"Last time someone saw her? Did someone report her missing?"

"Not that I know of; the po-po just showed up asking questions. I've been working double shifts the past week and I haven't seen her." I walked towards the building at the same time the police officers were coming out. They walked over to me and Jerome.

"Are you Alexis Harrington?"

"Yes, I am?"

"We were looking for you."

"Looking for me for what?" I asked.

"Are you the landlord?"

"Yes, is there something wrong?"

"Do you know Sia Jones?"

"Yes, she's a tenant here."

"How well did you know her?"

"I know her real well she was one of my first tenants when I bought the place."

"A body of a young woman was found near an abandoned farm. Her legs and arms were duct-taped and she was set on fire. We found her purse not too far from the body; the only thing in her purse was some keys and her driver's license with this address on it. We need you or the next of kin to come to the morgue to identify the body."

"I will come," I said. I looked at Jerome and said, "I'll be back soon. I pray this is not her."

"Me, too" Jerome replied.

When I arrived at the morgue I followed the police down a long corridor to a dark sterile room. The attendant removed the sheet from the body and I collapsed. It was Sia. Her body was burned badly, but her hair and the butterfly tattoo on her right ankle was untouched.

"Is this Sia Jones?" the officer asked.

"Yes, I remember seeing the butterfly on her ankle," I cried as I confirmed that she was Sia Jones.

"Do you have information for her next of kin?" the officer asked.

"I think she listed her mom as an emergency contact on her apartment application," I responded.

One of the officers supported my left arm as he led me out of the door. "Here is my card. Please call me with the information ASAP so we can notify her mother."

"I will send it to you as soon as I get back to the office," I said in a voice that was barely audible. I sat in my car and cried. My heart felt heavy, like someone was standing on it. I wondered who would want to hurt Sia? She was a young vibrant intelligent woman and her spirit was so sweet. I felt guilty for some reason. I couldn't help but think that her participation in SC Unite had something to do with her death. I drove back to the apartment complex in silence.

When I pulled into the parking lot I saw my sisters. They were standing in the parking lot with some of the other women and Jerome. I didn't have to say a word; the look on my face confirmed that the missing woman was Sia. I tried to talk; however, words would not come out. All I could say was, "It was her." I broke down in the parking lot. My sisters helped me inside the office. "I need Sia's mother's phone number so I can give it to the police." Autumn found her mother's number and handed it to me. My hands trembled as I dialed Lt. Davis' number. I couldn't stop crying enough for him to make out what I was saying, so Aubrey took the phone and gave him the number. I got up and laid on the black leather sofa and curled up in the fetal position and cried like a baby. That day I cried for Sia, for her family, the wounded child inside me, and any other women who had been hurt. When I gained my composure I asked Autumn to call Shamika. I couldn't talk to her, especially after having slept with Jason.

MARIAN

NO MATTER HOW CLEVERLY ALEXIS Harrington tried to hide her sordid organization, I found everything that I needed to know and more. I walked into the office of the apartment complex disguised as Side Chicks Unite, LLC and went off. "Side Chicks Unite? So you bitches are unified, huh? You are homewreckers and this nothing more than a fancy overpriced brothel."

"Excuse me?" Alexis said.

Ignoring her questions I continued ranting. "You think because you have rules that all these hoes abide by them?" I yelled.

"Mrs. Carey, either you calm down or you are going to have to leave."

"Oh, so you know who I am?" I smirked while giving her the relaxed bitch face.

"Yes, I do. I am sure we can discuss your accusations in a calm and rational manner, but your yelling is not going to help the situation." So this high yellow bitch thinks she is smart. I see she suffers from light-skinned syndrome.

She doesn't know me; I will set it off. I refused to calm down or de-escalate the situation. "Women like you make me sick! You use men for money and help them cheat."

"Men cheat because they want to cheat."

"It is whores like you that do not respect the sanctity of marriage. You bitches are fancy; your too good for a clandestine meeting once a week at a seedy motel where he leaves a few dollars on the nightstand and goes home to his family."

"You are absolutely right, Marian! For years women have been used by men for their own personal pleasure and they think if they take you out to dinner to Red Lobster they have done something big. I have no fucks left to give to a sorry-ass cheating dog-ass man."

I ignored her little diatribe as I looked around the well-decorated office. Well, one thing for sure: Madam Butterfly had expensive taste. "So you think this little fancy organization with an apartment complex full of tramps who demand that men pay all their bills, buy expensive cars, and pay for their education is not a brothel or prostitution?" I said while taking a seat at the conference table. I was in no rush to leave. I wanted her to know that I know all the ins and outs of her organization. Although one of her hoes was taking money out of my family household I had to respect the game. My sorry-ass husband has spent so much money on Shamika and her illegitimate unborn child I could file her on my taxes as a dependent. I looked straight into Alexis' piercing hazel eyes and said, "Ms. Alexis, I wonder what the community is going to think of you and your little prostitution ring. I see that donate to women's shelters and give scholarships with the money you make from the cheating men. Who do you think you are, Robin Hood? You take from the rich and give to the poor. I am going to make you pay. Your secret will be revealed to every news outlet and all over social media. Honey, you will definitely pay for destroying my family."

"Mrs. Carey, do what you feel you need to do. Just remember your husband is a part of this 'little organization,' as you call it. I know you want to live in the White House and I don't think you will jeopardize that because you crave power and fame."

I got up from the table and pushed the chair in. I looked at Alexis and said, "Madam Butterfly, you don't know me. Just watch me work."

ALEXIS

When Marian strutted out of my office I was perplexed. How did she know so much about the organization? All kinds of thoughts raced through my mind as I tried to figure out who told her. Where did the leak come from? Did Jason confess? Was it Shamika? I tried to talk to her and reason with her. I even reminded her of the non-disclosure form she signed. She was desperate to have Jason to herself so I wouldn't put anything past her. This girl was determined to have this baby she believed everything he told her about Marian: how she didn't understand or support him, the miscarriages, and her fertility problems. Shamika used this information and ran with it; somehow she saw that as divine intervention and believed that it was supposed to happen and they would live happily ever after. I should have broken my rule and kept him for myself.

Now I have to do damage control, if that's even possible. The media and social media will have a field day, especially Black Twitter. I can see the memes. I don't care about losing my job because with internet and satellite radio I can create my own show, which is something I've been thinking about doing lately. On mainstream radio black women never get a prime spot like the afternoon drive from 3:00 pm – 7:00 pm; they'd rather use men and sometimes corny ass comedians during rush hour.

I am concerned about my family; I have to protect Aubrey and Autumn. Then there is the possibility of jail. I am too cute to go to jail. Lord knows I don't want to be some butch girlfriend. I am willing to take the fall since SC Unite is my brainchild. Also, I had to protect the other men and women in the organization. Damn Shamika for catching feelings and not following protocol. I can't prove it, but I know that Shamika encouraged Sia to follow in her footsteps and now she is dead. Jerome told me about Malik coming to the apartment and how he heard them arguing and then Malik leaving in a hurry the other day. He also informed me that Shamika had been coming over to pick Sia up. Malik ain't shit; he didn't come to Sia's funeral. I didn't expect him to come, but he could have at least sent some flowers. This Negro had the nerve to send one of his flunkies to get her Jag before we put the girl in the ground and then called me and asked to meet another woman. This big-head bastard didn't seem to care that she was dead. I should have found a better way to protect my ladies, but I never thought this day would come.

ALEXIS

I FINALLY GOT A CHANCE to be a guest host during the afternoon drive; this is the spot I have been working for since I entered radio. I was going to do my thang so I would be asked back. The topic for the day was, "Is it okay for the man to cheat, but not the woman?" The callers were hot, especially the women. Many of them said things that made sense and others not so much. Most of the men who called in said the same thing, 'a man is just being a man.' A caller, Danny, said, "When a man does it (cheat) it has nothing to do with feelings; it's all about sex, but when a woman cheats she might have feelings for the other man and might leave." Another caller, Tonya, went off about the side chick or the jump-off. Her theory was that men can't cheat if they don't have anyone to cheat with. "Why is there no honor between women...no respect for other's relationships?" she asked. Since I was the only woman on the show the host let me answer, so I said, "The contract or commitment is between the man and the woman in the relationship. He knows he is married or in a relationship, so he should have enough restraint and respect for his woman that he will not cheat or invite that other energy into their relationship."

"This is true. I just think that women need to stick together since men can't control themselves" she said.

"I don't think that will ever happen. We have another caller. Caller, state your name and where you are calling from," the show's host said.

"Hi, my name is Gloria and I am calling from Alpharetta. I have a question."

"Go ahead with your question, Gloria," the host said.

"This question is for Alexis: what do you think about websites and organizations that help men cheat?" I turned beet red. Although she said her name was Gloria, I knew it was Marian. I recognized her voice from her confrontation in the office.

I cleared my throat and said, "Men have been cheating since the beginning of time and if there is an organization that is willing to capitalize on their actions, I have no judgments."

"How would you feel if you were married and your husband was a part of this type of organization?"

"Well, Gloria, if I was married I guess I would be hurt. But, I can't control his actions."

"Well, my man is a part of this organization called Side Chicks Unite and he got his little side chick pregnant."

"Whoa!" all the men in the studio said in unison. "Side Chicks Unite? Where is this organization?" the host asked.

"It's right here in our backyard. Isn't that right, Alexis?" Everyone turned and looked at me. I just gave them a blank stare. I knew this was going to go bad. *Fuck it, I might as well own my shit.*

"As a matter of fact, it is," I said.

"Of course it is; you are the ringleader. Tell them, Madam Butterfly, how you help my husband and so many other men, powerful, rich men, cheat on their wives for money. Tell them about your little brothel in East Point."

"We will be back after this break," the host said and the station went to commercial.

VANESSA

LOOK AT GOD! MY GRANDMOTHER used to say the Lord will always leave a ram in the bush. I could shout up and down my street. I am willing to bet Aubrey took the money from the church and gave it to her sister to open her little brothel in East Point. The caller just outed Alexis on the radio. They hurried up and went to commercial. All I have to do is prove that the $300,000 that Aubrey transferred to her personal account went to her sister. This is too good to be true. Once I confirm where the money went I will put together a video to show during the bishop's anniversary celebration. I sent Aubrey another text: Let the wicked forsake his ways.

AUTUMN

I ALMOST CRASHED MY CAR when Gloria confronted Alexis on the radio. I knew it was Jason's wife using a fake name. I guess she didn't want to reveal her husband's identity. I called Alexis immediately, but her phone went to voice mail. As soon as I was ending the call my phone beeped and it was Aubrey. "Hello," I answered.

"Girl, were you listening to the radio?"

"Yes!"

"Please don't tell me that Gloria is really Marian," Bre said.

"Yes, it was her," I responded.

"I tried calling Alexis, but I keep getting her voicemail."

"Me too, Bre. I don't know if she is still on the air or if she has left the station."

"Damn, this is a mess..." Aubrey stated and then her voice trailed off and she became silent. I could tell she was deep in thought. She always stops midsentence when she is lost for words.

"I had a feeling that this day would come, but not so soon. Hell, I was getting ready to leave Sodom and Gomorrah."

"Girl, we have bigger worries than you leaving a job you hate. What if they try to arrest us for prostitution? Or how am I going to explain this to Kai? I haven't even paid the church back their money," Aubrey said frantically.

"The church their money?! What the hell did you do, Bre?!"

"I kind of borrowed the money from the church to help Alexis buy the apartment complex."

"Why y'all didn't tell me?"

"We just felt that it was better if you didn't know." How in the world are we going to fix this? I thought. The scandal of setting married men up with single women was one thing, but taking the money from the church is another. "Don't worry, Bre, we will figure this out. I'm headed to the office now." I ended the call.

ALEXIS

THAT BITCH HAD THE NERVE to call the radio station. The phones were ringing off the hook after Gloria's call and Twitter and Facebook were on fire. I had ten missed calls - two from Autumn, and the rest from Aubrey. I sent a group text to Autumn and Aubrey and asked them to meet me at the office.

I called Jason; he was listening to the show and confirmed that it was his wife's voice. We tried to figure out how she knew about the organization. *I'm glad I fucked her husband. Once the smoke clears I might just take him from her.* I'd been so busy with trying to deal with Sia's death and making sure the rest of the women were protected I'd forgotten to tell Jason about Marian's visit. I wonder if Shamika said anything to her. "Do you think Shamika told her about the organization?" I asked.

"I honestly don't know."

"I didn't get a chance to call and tell you this, but Marian came into my office and showed out."

"When? Why didn't you tell me the day it happened?"

"I was going to...I thought I had time to tell you. I didn't think she would do something like this."

"Me, neither. I was going to stay with her; however, after this little stunt, I can't be with a woman who is so vindictive."

"You were going to stay? What about Mika? How were you going to explain to her that you were staying with your wife?"

"The day after you left the loft I spoke to Shamika and I told her that I wasn't sure if I was going to leave because I want to be Vice-President."

"What did she say?"

"Of course, she was not happy. I told her I needed some time."

I wished I was close to him; I would slap the shit out of him for playing with that little girl's heart. I wouldn't be surprised if she did call Marian and tell her that she's pregnant. He is a typical man, always thinking with his little head instead of his big head. I can't give him any more of my energy. I ended the call just as I pulled into the parking lot of SC Unite. The last person I wanted to see was Jerome. He looked at me like he wanted to say something, but the look on my face let him know I was in no mood for gossip. "Hi, Jerome," I said, waving my hand and hurrying into the building. "Hello, Ms. Alexis," he responded and got on the golf cart.

When I walked into my office Autumn and Aubrey were there. Autumn was drinking a glass of wine and Aubrey was drinking Apple Crown Royal on the rocks. Aubrey was nervous and falling apart at the seams.

"What are we going to do?" Aubrey asked.

"Like I told y'all before...I am going to protect you both so whatever happens, happens."

"You know Mom called. She said one of her church members was listening to the radio," Aubrey said. I could give two fucks about her church members; besides why are they listening to a secular radio station? Shouldn't they be listening to the gospel station? Well, she didn't call me and I hope she doesn't."

"You know she is not going to call you," Autumn said.

"Good...'cause I don't need a sermon right now." I am sure she is worried about what her friends and the rest of her snooty family is going to say. My feelings or actions are not tied to their opinions. I poured a glass of wine and rubbed my temple. My head was throbbing from the lack of food and today's events. "You two didn't know anything about what I was doing. As far as you know we were renting property and I was using the money to help in the community," I stated. Both my sisters looked like two deer caught in headlights. "Do you two understand the words that are coming out of my mouth? I need to hide all the financial records except the receipts for rent payments."

Aubrey took a sip of her drink and said, "We can hide them in my safe at the church."

"Are you sure you want to do this?" I asked. "We have used the church enough."

"Listen, we are in this together."

"We still have to pay the church back...damn, I thought we would have some more time," I said. I couldn't help but be pissed at Shamika's stanking ass for getting pregnant. I know that started this little whirlwind. I have to meet with the rest of the women and the sponsors. I still have to protect their identities. I had a headache out of this world. I could say fuck it, take the money I have and leave the country. But, sink or swim I will ride this storm out.

SHAMIKA

WHEN AUTUMN CALLED ME AND told me about Sia's death I lost control. I let out a blood-curdling scream. My world came tumbling down that day. Damn, who would want to kill my girl? She was my best friend; we were closer than me and my biological sisters. I felt guilty. I shouldn't have had her pretend to be pregnant in an attempt to get Malik to leave his wife. Although Malik was a multi-millionaire he was still hood and had some seedy people in his entourage. I bet my life that he had something to do with her death. The day I picked her up to go with me to yoga class she told me that he demanded that she get an abortion or he would stomp the baby out of her.

Now that she was gone I was alone. I had no one to talk to or confide in. She promised me that she would be with me throughout my pregnancy and accompany me to my doctor appointments and to Lamaze class; until Jason could. He's trying to use what Alexis said as an excuse to go back on his word, talking about he don't trust me and now he's got to think about leaving his wife. So I had to take matters into my own hands. That's why I sent Marian a picture of the positive pregnancy test and I sent her a Facebook message explaining how we met. If he is not going to leave on his own I'm sure having a baby outside his marriage will make her leave, especially if she is not woman enough to give him any babies. I am not to be messed with.

MARIAN

LOVE AND MONEY ARE THE two greatest reasons to kill. I befriended this home-wrecking hussy at *Oh Baby Fitness* a yoga class for expectant mothers. I bought a custom-made prosthetic pregnant belly; it was very comfortable and it looked and felt like real skin. Shamika was so talkative. Although she did not come out and say she was pregnant by my husband she did reveal that she was pregnant by a married man and due to his high profile she had to keep their relationship a secret. The little tramp didn't know that I was the wife that she sent the picture of the pregnancy test to and the Facebook message. She is so dumb. This bitch even told me that he pays all her living expense. I already knew this because I hired a private detective to follow him.

How dare she cheat with my husband and not use protection? I know her type; she probably got pregnant on purpose. I know my husband has loose lips and probably told her that I cannot have a baby. She is trying to take my place. That will not happen.

I'm so glad that I knew the backup password to his phone since it's password-protected with his fingerprint. Jason has cheated on me before. The first time I caught him he was at the booty club all hugged up with some young girl; when I walked up on them he turned pale. He was sweating like a bear trying to explain. We went to counseling and decided we would make things work and now he's at it again. Normally, whenever he cheated on me it was always with a young light-skinned bitch with long hair. This hussy had weave and she was not as light as the others, but lighter than me. I'm stuck in the middle. I'm too dark to be light-skinned and too light to be dark-skinned. He loves women with long hair. When we met I had shoulder-length hair and when I got it cut he had a fit, so to be spiteful I kept my hair cut as short as Toni Braxton. I am not the model type, but I am attractive and petite.

I don't know why or how I have stayed with Jason's cheating ass for this long. He doesn't deserve me. I held him down when he was in law school, making sure we had food to eat and paying all the bills because he was a broke student on financial aid. When my parents refused to give me money I worked two jobs to make sure the rent was paid and the lights were on in our first apartment. After he graduated and passed the bar exam he was offered a job with a prestigious law firm in downtown Atlanta. He wanted to be a civil rights lawyer, but I encouraged him to go into corporate law; that's when he changed. I bought him expensive suites, dress shirts, and shoes with the money I received from my inheritance when my grandfather died. It was enough money to change our lives. My parents did not approve of Jason and wanted me to marry my high school sweetheart, David Baker. They felt Jason was not good enough for me because his family was poor. We rarely spent time with my family. We stopped going to Connecticut for holidays because Jason felt uncomfortable. I would always go visit by myself. All the sacrifices I made to be with him and he repays me by getting some tramp pregnant.

When Jason came home I was watching television in the family room. He barely spoke as he headed upstairs. I know he doesn't love me anymore and it hurts. The way he looks at me and refuses to touch me is a telltale sign that this marriage is over and we are just sharing a space. Trying to get pregnant put a strain on our relationship. We used to be so happy and in love. "Jason," I said.

"Yeah," he replied.

"Can we talk?" I asked.

"What's up?"

I exhaled and said, "I know you want to have a child and I am sorry I can't have one, but we can adopt." He turned around and looked at me like I had two heads. "You can't possibly think that having a baby is going to fix everything?"

"No, I don't think a baby will fix everything. I know I was against adoption at first but I realize there are a lot of children who need a good home."

"I don't want to discuss this right now. I am trying to focus on my career," he said.

"I know how important your career is to you; don't forget I've helped you get to where you are." I struggled to remain composed. The last thing I wanted to do was to get into an argument with Jason. I needed him to be on board with adopting or else my plans will be wrecked.

"You don't make me happy...I am not in love with you and having a baby is not going to change that, and Marian, I don't want to bring a child into this type of home." I could not believe what he just said. I couldn't move. I tried to speak, but the words would not come out. He finally told the truth. He must love this little bitch. I am going to make his life miserable until 'death do us part'. His death.

VANESSA

I FOUND OUT THAT AUBREY gave her dear sweet sister Madam Alexis a cashier's check for $300,000. I called the bank and pretended to be her to verify that the check had been cashed. So this trifling heffa stole money from the church to help her sister open up a brothel. She was going to hell on an express train. I hope she enjoyed the ride. My heart was overjoyed at the thought that I would cause her as much pain as she has caused me. Her perfect life will be destroyed. I have a sex tape of us that will be shown in church for the bishop's anniversary.

AUBREY

I KNEW DEEP DOWN THAT starting Side Chicks Unite was not a good idea; however, my desire for revenge overrode common sense. I'm happy that I was able to help my sisters and working with them has been great, so if we have to share a cell together then so be it. My only regret is that I used the church's money. Autumn brought me the external drive with all of our clients' information: we had their financial information, health records, and payment receipts for their side chick. After I locked the drive in the church safe I was ready for our final meeting for the planning of Kai's anniversary. The text messages had stopped as abruptly as they began. Edith was happy with the bank statement and hadn't asked about the statement for the benevolence funds, so even if another storm was brewing at least this one had died down.

When I walked into the conference room all eyes were on me, which wasn't unusual - I am fabulous like that - yet this time was different. The tension in the room was thick. Vanessa's and my eyes locked and I could see the disdain she had for me. She smiled. I gave her the resting bitch face look and sat down. "Good morning, ladies. I am so glad to see you all this morning. I hope all is well with you today," I said.

When everyone spoke in unison and I could tell something was wrong. I wondered how many of them had heard the radio show. By now Side Chicks Unite was all over the news, Facebook, and Twitter. Alexis was referred to as a madam. The City of East Point police had called Alexis in for questioning. She hadn't been charged with anything for now. As far as they were concerned she was just the landlord of an apartment complex.

They interviewed the women and each one denied being connected to a brothel or prostitution ring. They were just renters. All of them had jobs or were full-time students. One of the rules of the organization was that you had to be productive and have goals and strive to reach those goals.

Ms. Mary was the first to speak. "Let us join hands and pray so we can get down to the business at hand," she said. "Dear Father God, we come to you this day with a troubled heart. Lord, you know the Devil is busy and he is on the attack. We ask that you provide covering for the bishop and the first lady during these difficult times, Father God. We pray for the first lady's sister, Father God. Lord Jesus, we don't know if what they say in the media is true but we know that you know. We ask that you be the judge and juror because only you can judge, Father God. We come to you this day on bended knee with humility in our hearts and spirit, Father God, as we ask that you keep the blood of Jesus over the first lady's family."

"Amen," everyone said. Ms. Mary wobbled over to me and gave me a hug. For an eighty-year-old woman she was still sharp.

"Thank you, Sister Mary, for that heartfelt prayer," I said as we embraced.

"I am not on Space Book and I don't listen to the news - just too much bad information." I chuckled when she called Facebook – Space book. "I just trust God and I know all is well in the universe. I heard tell that your sister Alexis was running a brothel. I don't know, that's what they say," she said.

"My sister is not running a brothel," I said loudly. Most of the women dropped their heads to avoid making eye contact with me. I knew they were gossiping before I walked in and now you could hear a rat piss on cotton. "Well, let's get started with the meeting." I'll be so glad when anniversary celebration is over so I don't have to meet with these fake-ass church folks anymore.

ALEXIS

DAMN, WHAT A WEEK. I am under investigation for being a madam, I was fired from the radio station, and my mother has disowned me. I expected that much from her - our relationship has been strained for years. How dare I tarnish her good name? It is times like this, I miss my grandmother. Mommy Dearest called me ranting, talking about, "I cannot believe you! Do you know what people are saying about you? I am so embarrassed that my oldest child is involved in a prostitution ring. They are calling you the Madam of East Point. I am just ashamed to show my face at my sorority meeting. I hope you didn't involve Autumn in your foolishness. I know Aubrey is a mighty woman of God and is too smart to get involved with your shenanigans!" I guess she called herself getting me straight. I wasn't disrespectful. I quietly listened but her words went in one ear and out of the other. I can give two fucks about what she thinks or anyone else in the family; they really can kiss the center part of my ass. One thing she doesn't need to worry about is Autumn and Aubrey. I will make sure their names are not linked to Side Chicks Unite, LLC.

My father's call was totally different from my mother's over-the-top, always caring about what people say bougie ass. He didn't believe a word that was said about his little angel. He told me, "I don't give a rat's ass what people say. I know my baby is not a madam or a prostitute. If you need a lawyer let me know. I know people." I love my dad; he always has my back. The calls kept coming in and I let them go to voicemail. I avoided social media because people can be so cruel; especially on Black Twitter they will say anything when they are hiding behind their computer, laptops, or smartphones...damn keyboard warriors. Jason called and I wanted to cuss him out for going raw into Shamika's dumb ass. I can't put all the blame on him because I hired her.

"Hello," I mumbled.

"So, Madam Butterfly, how are you holding up?" he joked.

"Oh, so you think this is a game? You don't care about my freedom."

"No, baby, I don't want you to go to jail. You are too pretty to go to jail and be some big strong woman's girlfriend."

"Baby? Don't you have enough babies?" I hissed.

"You are the only one that counts."

"Really? What about you, Shamika, and your unborn child and living happily ever after?"

"She is too young and has a lot of growing up to do. I need a more mature woman."

"You have one...she's your wife, or have you forgotten?"

"No, I haven't. She is the same age as me, but she is not mature. No mature woman would call a radio station with allegations and not be woman enough to reveal their true identity. Now you have been fired and your name dragged through the mud. She doesn't have the guts to tell me that she knows; therefore, I don't know what else she is planning. Plus, she had the nerve to say let's adopt a baby in hopes that it will save our marriage. I told her no and that a baby is not going to save our marriage, and that I refuse to bring a baby into a loveless house. I don't love her anymore."

"Damn, Jay, you said all that?"

"Yes!" I was silent. He had more balls than I gave him credit for. I thought he was Marian's little puppet.

"Alexis, I got you. I know people in high places. You will come out of this unscathed. Trust me." *Trust him? Shit! I don't trust anyone but myself and my sisters.* He must have been reading my mind because he said, "Alexis, you can trust me. I promise I will make all this go away."

MARIAN

JASON'S WORDS CUT LIKE A knife, but he is not as skilled as cutting as I am. I'm sure once he sees the baby he will change his mind. I know he will. After all, I have been here for him through thick and thin and that has got to count for something. I was his ride or die. I went against my family to be with him. I am not giving up my husband. Alexis destroyed my family; if she wouldn't have introduced my husband to that young tramp I wouldn't be going through all this. No one knows that I am Gloria. He should be thanking me that I am still protecting his lying cheating ass. His dumb ass doesn't even know that I know he has a baby on the way.

Oh my God, what if Alexis told Jason that I confronted her? Oh shit, Marian...think think think. I should have played it cool. Why do you do dumb shit on impulse? It's okay; he hasn't said anything...think think think. I have to find out how much he knows. I got to get rid of the little tramp and get her...our baby. I shouldn't have had the detective I hired to follow him around killed. I have to find out what he knows.

JASON

I HAD TO HELP ALEXIS she wouldn't be going through this if I hadn't gotten Shamika pregnant. She was being crucified in the media and on social media. I told her I would get her out of this mess, so I have to. I called my boy, Lawrence Hunter, the one person I knew who could make this situation go away. Lawrence was originally from Jamaica, but had some strong connections with people in politics, the entertainment industry, and just about anything else. If someone owed you money all you had to do was call Lawrence and he would send who he called "collectors" to visit them and they would get your money. Lawrence hated when I referred to the "collectors" as the Jamaican mafia. "What's up, frat? I need a favor."

"Anything for you, bruh," Lawrence said.

"You heard about the Madam of East Point?"

"Yeah...man, who hasn't. That shit is all over the news, Facebook, Twitter, and Instagram. I heard they are trying to find out who her clients are and word on the street is she had some powerful men on her roster. First, that dating website for married people got hacked and now this. Damn, a married man can't get a little piece of ass on the side in secret anymore."

"Who is 'they,' bruh?"

"They...the media...TMZ. Hell, inquiring minds want to know."

"I know her personally. She is a close personal friend of mine. Man, I need to make this go away." I put an emphasis on 'personal' so he would know she is more than just a friend.

My boy was silent for a minute and then he said, "Oh, 'personal.' I get it."

"Are you sure? You acting kind of slow today. You still smoking that medicinal weed?"

"Yes, I need it for my cataracts...I have migraines...I'm stressed," he busted out laughing.

"Man, you're still a fool!" I laughed. This dude always got jokes. He was a clown in college. But he was always one hundred grand. Lawrence was 6'9", non-muscular, and dark-skinned. He had two nicknames; before we pledged people referred to him as Biggie Smalls and on the line our big brother named him Smoke because of his skin color.

"What you need, bruh? I got you!"

"I need this to go away."

"Man, let me ask you this - is she a madam? She pimpin' these hoes?"

"Man, she is not a madam and she is not pimping anyone...she owns an apartment complex in East Point and she rents out the apartments. She is a landlord."

"Sure, she is...so why did some woman clown her on the radio the other day? I heard the sound bites." I sighed I wanted to tell my boy everything. I couldn't say it over the phone.

"I think she is being framed, so I am trying to help the sister out...she is good people."

"Bet that, bruh...I will see what I can do." He knew I couldn't say what I wanted on the phone so he asked, "What are you doing for lunch?"

"I think I'm going to get some Ackee Salt Water Fish, Callou, and a beef patty," I said. "Bet that, I got a taste for some ox tails. I'll meet you at the spot at 1:00," Lawrence said. Whenever one of us described Jamaican food we knew we needed to meet in person.

I was developing feelings for Alexis. I low-key blame Alexis; if she would have agreed to be my girlfriend when we first met we probably wouldn't be going through this. I did get her in the bed and I want her in my bed again, so I got to keep her out of jail. Hindsight is fifty-fifty. I now know that Mika was on a mission to find a husband so she could live the life of a socialite. She thought the baby would trap me and I must admit she almost did.

MARIAN

I NEEDED TO FIND SOMEONE to get rid of Jason's bitch. I know for sure that Jason knows that I know about his situation and that I was the one who called the radio station. I was told that Lawrence Hunter, his fraternity brother, called in favors from everybody: the Mayor, Chief of Police, the District Attorney's office, and a few judges and the investigation ended. Lawrence Hunter is a male version of Olivia Pope he knows how to clean up or stop a scandal. And Jason is his brother from another mother; those two are thick as thieves so Lawrence will do anything for him.

Jason's reputation was still intact and he was ready to hit the campaign trail in a few months, and his daughter and I will join him. I don't really care about Alexis; she can keep doing what she is doing. I just wanted her to know that I knew.

I needed to get rid of Jason's tramp after she has our baby. So, I called my first cousin Malik; we grew up together. He moved in with us when he was thirteen years old after his parents died in a car crash, so we were more like brother and sister than cousins. He was kind of hood when he moved in with us and even though he is a multimillionaire he is still kind of hood and he always has a bunch of thugs hanging around him. I scrolled through my IPhone 6 and found his number.

"What up, cuz?" Malik said.

"Not too much, just trying to make it," I responded.

"Long time no hear from. How is everybody doing?"

"Everyone is good," I said.

"What you need, cuz? I know you didn't call a nigga just to say hi."

My skin cringed when he used the N-word. Why does he have to talk like that? He went to the finest private schools and yet he talks like he is from the projects.

"I need a favor," I replied.

"What you need?"

"I have a problem that I need to go away."

"What kind of problem? That Bama ain't messing with you is he? You know we will ride up on him."

"Jason and I are fine," I rolled my eyes.

"What it do...what you need, big cuz? I got you."

"I need...well, Jason had an affair and I...you know."

"No, I don't know. You want me to handle him?"

"No, I need you to handle her."

"Ok...that's what's up? What's her name and where does she live?"

"Her name is Shamika Matthews. She lives at 7200 Hillandale Rd in Atlanta."

"Did you say Shamika?"

"Yes, why? Do you know her?"

"Is she pregnant?"

"Yes, How did you know?"

"She was friends with someone I knew."

"It's a small world. I need her to disappear after she has the baby."

"Yes, it is a small world...I can't stand that bitch!" He snapped.

"Good, then we have a common enemy. I'll let you know when she has her baby. Call me when you pick her up."

"We got you, cuz! We will call you when we pick her ass triflin' ass up."

"Thank you cuz." I said and ended the call.

JASON

SHAMIKA WAS BLOWING MY CELL phone up again. She was not happy when I told her it was over. How could she think that I would want to be with her after she sent a copy of the pregnancy stick to Marian and told her that we met through Side Chicks Unite? I guess she thought that would force Marian to divorce me, but what she didn't know is that Marian cared more about her image, status, and my political career than anything in this world and if push came to shove she will protect it at all costs. I am done with both of them. I am tired of conniving women in my life and they have to go. Marian is disillusioned if she thinks we are going to adopt a child. Nothing could be further from my mind. How did I get involved with two crazy-ass women? I am batting a thousand.

Shamika is spoiled and wanted everything her way. Her downfall was that she couldn't hold water. In a heated discussion she yelled, "You think you slick, you think you can get me pregnant and not keep your promise. You must think I'm slow, but let me tell you something, 'Mr. I'm concentrating on my political career,' you won't have one because I sent your wife a picture of the pregnancy test, the ultrasound, and told her how we met. So marinate on that, Mr. Lover Lover!" She was in full black woman mode, complete with the neck roll and finger-pointing. Her confession let me know that Marian knew.

After her rant I said, "This relationship is over. I will pay child support; I want a relationship with my child, but not with you." I took the keys to her apartment off my key ring, looked her in the eyes, and said, "I will pay the rent for the rest of the year, so you and my child will have a roof over your head and you can keep the car, but you will not get another dime from me unless it is for my child." I got up, walked to the door, and turned around and said, "Call me when you have it," and walked out. Ending my relationship with Shamika brought me peace. Now all I had to do is end my marriage.

I got in my truck and called Alexis. "What's up, Jay?"

"You tell me."

"I'm just sitting in my office writing a treatment for my own Internet radio show."

"Good for you."

"To what do I owe the honor of this call?"

"I was thinking about you."

"Oh yeah, what were you thinking? Good things, I hope."

"Well, Madam Butterfly, I was thinking about how soft your lips felt and I wished I could kiss them right now."

"Whet?" she laughed. No, she didn't hit me with the ghetto grammar.

I went into my slang vernacular, "Yea shawty...no, what umm sayin'" and we both laughed. Talking to Alexis was easy; she was like a homie. I could be silly with her. Damn, I could be myself.

"Well, I guess I do owe you a meal or something, since you kept me from being sent up the river."

I smiled, "Why, yes you do, and a brother is a little hungry."

"Me too...I swear I am hungrier than a hostage. I feel like my stomach is touching my back."

"Girl, let's go get some groceries."

"Cool," she responded.

"I'm on my way to get you."

"Okay, I'll be waiting," she said seductively. I turned the volume up on the radio and sang along to R. Kelly's "You Bring Me Joy" and headed towards her office.

SHAMIKA

MY EYES WERE RED AND swollen from crying. I couldn't make the tears stop falling. I absolutely had no one. My best friend in the world, Sia, was dead and now the love of my life doesn't want to be with me. My heart ached. I wanted the world to know that Congressman Jason Carey was my baby daddy. All of the trips and weekend getaways to place like Tybee Island, Charleston, SC, Blue Ridge Mountains, and Cozumel and I didn't have any pictures of us together. I didn't have any proof that we'd spent time together.

How could he do this to me? I know my child will be taken care of financially, but I don't want to be a single parent. I want a husband...I want him. I needed someone to talk to, so at last I called my mother. "Hi, Mom," I said.

"Hey, baby. How you doin'?"

"I'm doing all right. I was just calling to check on you."

"I'm doing all right. I just got off the phone with Gladys; you know she more saved than the rest of us." I started laughing. My aunt Gladys is a mess - let her tell it she has a direct line to Jesus. It is times like this when I miss my family.

"What Auntie do now?" I asked.

"The same ole same ole. I get tired of her calling me with mess and then start preaching and acting like she's speaking in tongues. At least she didn't come over here with that damn olive oil trying to convince people that it's holy oil." I started laughing I remember when I spent the night with her all of us would wake up with oil on our forehead.

"Mama, you talk to Daddy?"

"Child, no! We cordial when we see each other at church, but I don't have a lot of words for him."

"I wish y'all could have worked it out."

"Baby, there comes a time when you have to love yourself more than you love anyone else. If you keep giving a man chances and he keeps doing the same thing, especially when he's over fifty, it's time to let his ass go." What my mom said made sense but made me sad at the same time. I knew in my heart that I had to let Jason go. If he cheated on his wife with me, then he would probably cheat on me with someone else. If he already hadn't. "Baby, what's wrong? You don't sound like yourself...you sound sad," my mother asked.

"Nothing, I'm just tired. The baby should be here any day now."

"I'm so excited! I can't wait to see my grand youngin'! You want me to come up there a few days so I can be at the hospital with you? I got plenty of vacation time."

"No, Mom...my fiancé is going to be at the hospital with me. You can come to the house when we get home I will call you."

"Fiancé? This is the first I heard tell of a fiancé. When you get a fiancé?"

"Mom, I got engaged last week."

"Well, congratulations, I guess...I just want to be there when you have the baby...my baby is having a baby and I want to be at the hospital. Plus I want to meet this fiancé." I had to end this call before my mom started asking more questions. I could tell by the way she kept saying fiancé that she didn't believe me. My mother always knew when I was lying. I couldn't get away with shit growing up. I needed to lie down. I was starting to feel pain in my lower back, which probably came from me cleaning all day and organizing the baby's nursery.

"Mom, I'm starting to get a little sleepy so I am going to lie down for a while. I will call you from the hospital after I have the baby."

"Well, I'm coming to the hospital after you have it. I'm going to stay for a couple of days. I don't care what you say, so tell your fiancé." I knew there was no point in arguing with Jean Ann.

"Okay, Mom. I love you!"

"I love you too, baby!" No matter what I am going through talking to my mom always puts me in a better mood. I laughed out loud thinking about my aunt Gladys. I felt the urge to use the bathroom for the hundredth time today and as soon as I made it to the bathroom I felt a gush of water. I panicked; I didn't know what to do, so I called Autumn - she has a daughter. I was afraid she wouldn't answer my call or hang up as soon as she heard my voice, so when she said hello, I quickly said, "Hi Autumn, this is Shamika my water just broke and I don't know what to do!" I felt a contraction so strong it caused me to double over in pain.

"Hang up and call 911 and tell them that you are in labor and your water just broke, and then call me back." I called 911 and then immediately called Autumn back.

"I just called 911. They are on the way."

"Great, what hospital are you going to?"

"I'm supposed to have my baby at Northside."

"Okay, I am going to stay on the phone with you until the ambulance gets there. Once they arrive ask them where they are taking you, so I can meet you there." I was stunned that she was willing to do that for me. I cried. After all I had done to her sister and their organization and she was still willing to help me. The ambulance arrived about ten minutes later. "Autumn, they are taking me to Northside."

"I will meet you there."

AUTUMN

When Shamika called to tell me that her water had broken and she didn't know what to do, I knew she needed my help. We hadn't spoken since I told her about Sia's death. She was so distraught at the funeral that she had to be carried out. I didn't go to the burial site or the repass. I just wanted to pay my respects. Sia was a sweet girl.

I was surprised the media didn't try to tie her death to SC Unite. After Marian called the radio station there was so much gossip and speculation. I expected there to be more fallout from it, but Jason told Alexis he would take care of it and he did. Aubrey's and my name were never mentioned, and I felt so bad for Lexi - she took all the negative press and gossip like a trooper. I really admired her strength.

I felt sorry for Shamika; she was alone and it can be scary to go through childbirth and not have anyone with you. If it wasn't for Alexis I would have had Morgan by myself when I was stationed at Fort Sam Houston, Texas. I was grateful my sister flew in from Detroit to be by my side. In a way Shamika was still our little sister, a hard-headed sister, and we would always be connected by SC Unite.

When I arrived at Northside Hospital Shamika had dilated to eight centimeters. The contractions were less than five minutes apart. Lying in the hospital bed she looked like a helpless child. I sat down next to her and took her hand. She damn near broke my fingers when the contraction hit. She was hollering and cussing like a sailor. I understood her struggle; I'd been there done that. The nurses were trying to get her to calm down. "Look at me, Shamika," I said.

"It hurt so bad, please get it out!" she screamed.

"Did you take Lamaze classes?" She didn't answer; she just nodded her head. "Okay, then I need you to breathe like they taught you in Lamaze."

"Fuck Lamaze...I can't remember that bullshit right now! It hurts so bad...oh shit, here comes another one!!!"

"It has been an hour. I need to check you again to see how far you are now," the nurse said.

Shamika started crying. "It hurts so bad...can I get some drugs?"

"Yes, you can get an epidural," the nurse said.

"Yes, give me drugs," Shamika pleaded.

"You are at nine centimeters. It won't be too much longer. I will be back with the medicine," the nurse said and walked out of the room.

"Autumn, did you have an epidural?"

"No, I was scared. I heard a lot or horror stories about it so I had a natural childbirth. It hurt like hell. I guess that's why I only have one child.'

"This is my last child. I can't do this shit no more. I don't know how my mom had seven kids." We both laughed.

I texted Lexi: Shamika is in labor I'm at Northside with her now.

Alexis texted back: K...I'm with her baby daddy right now.

What? I replied.

We are having dinner and then I am going to be his dessert...lol

SMH...I'll text you when the little bundle of joy arrives, I texted and then put my phone on silent.

Sia LaShay Matthews was born at 10:59 pm; she weighed seven pounds five ounces and was seventeen inches long, and she was absolutely beautiful. She looked white, like a lot of African-American children when they are first born, but their ears are a little darker, which lets you know what their skin complexion will be when their color fills in. From the looks of her ears she will have Jason's medium-brown skin tone. This child had a head full of black curly hair and a set of lungs that could wake the dead.

My eyes teared up when I saw the look in Shamika's eyes, I knew this little girl would change her and hopefully for the better. I watched her cry as she snuggled up with her baby girl. "Thank you, Autumn, for being here for me."

"You are welcome."

"I appreciate it. None of the other ladies in SC Unite will talk to me. I don't blame them. I was awful and what I did to Alexis was awful. She treated me like a sister and I stabbed her in the back. So again, thank you."

"Again, you are welcome. Shamika, we all make mistakes. We just have to learn from our mistakes, forgive others and ourselves, and move on."

"You sound like my mother...she doesn't hold grudges for nothing. She will forgive anyone. I need to call her." The nurse came and got little Sia and took her to the nursery. I took this as my queue to leave.

"I will let you get some rest. Do you need anything before I go?"

"No, thank you...will you come back tomorrow?"

"Yes, I will, call me if you need me to bring you anything. Also, I will give you a ride home if you need it."

"I will let you know. My mom said she could come and stay with us for a few days."

"All right, sweetie...get some rest and I will be back tomorrow." When I got to my car I texted Lexi: <u>Tell Shamika's baby's daddy that his little girl has arrived...her name is Sia LaShay.</u>

MARIAN

PEOPLE LOVE TO PUT THEIR business on Facebook and then get mad when someone makes a comment that they don't like. Right after Shamika gave birth she posted a picture of herself and her new baby in the hospital with the caption, "My bundle of joy has arrived...she is my heartbeat... my world. Welcome to the world Sia LaShay Matthews." I can't believe she named her child after her dead friend. This is too much. We haven't talked since I attended her baby shower. I guess in a few days I have to go get my daughter.

VANESSA

D-DAY WAS FINALLY HERE. I woke up extra early so I could get to the church and switch the video. Yesterday's family day was a success; the members and their families had so much fun at the picnic. It was great to see everyone fellowshipping together. We had a moon walk, water slides, face painting, Disney characters, a pony, and plenty of food and other activities. Kai and Aubrey looked like a happy couple as they watched KJ play.

Aubrey walked up to me and gave me a big hug and said, "Thank you, Vanessa, for all your hard work; everything is wonderful." I almost changed my mind about showing the video. She sounded so sincere.

"You are welcome," I replied. It felt good to feel her arms around me. I welcomed her embrace. I didn't want to let her go. I loved the smell of one of her favorite perfumes, Jimmy Choo Flash, she smelled so good. It reminded me of times when we were happy. I drove past her house almost every day. I still loved her very much, and not being with her was killing me slowly. I couldn't sleep. I couldn't eat. I missed her - I just wished I could get her out of my mind. I felt bad that Kai would be hurt and embarrassed, but sometimes the innocent have to suffer with the bad.

Edith startled me when I entered the media room. "Oh! Good morning, Sister Edith, I didn't expect to see you here this early."

"I'm sorry if I startled you, Sister Vanessa. I needed to make sure the video was queued for service this morning."

"Great minds think alike. I was doing the same thing." Damn, she messed up my plans. I had to get rid of her so I could switch the video.

Edith got on my nerves; the biggest mistake I made was befriending this fashion misfit. She was useless to me now. Damn, now I had to go back to the media room and switch the video without being seen. "Is there anything else that needs to be done, Sister Edith?"

"No, don't think so."

I looked in my handbag like I was looking for something important. "I forgot my Bible; let me run to my car to see if I left it there."

"You can look on mine if you would like."

"Thank you, sister, but I like to highlight scriptures and make notes. I will meet you in the choir room."

"I can walk with you. We still have time before we have to line up." I couldn't shake this loser and I was getting agitated. "Sister, you don't have to walk back outside with me; it's drizzling a little bit and I wouldn't want your hair to get wet."

"No problem, I have my umbrella...see?" she said, holding it up.

"Bless your heart, you are so sweet," I smiled. "Let's go, sister, before it pours down. The sky is looking kind of dark."

The sky was a dark grey just like my mood. I took long strides as I walked. Edith was right on my heel. The whole time she was talking non-stop. The more she talked the more irritated I became. Today is the day that I reveal First Lady Aubrey's secrets and this chatterbox was standing in the way. I needed to switch the video.

When we got back inside we went to the choir room. I was relieved when Brother Twuan, the choir director, started talking to Edith about her solo. She might look like a ragamuffin, but she can sing. While she was talking to "Twuan the Don," as everyone called him, I slipped out and hurried down to the media room. Gary, the sound guy, was in there. Damn, I couldn't catch a break. "Hi Gary, I just wanted to make sure everything was good with the video."

"Terrance is not here yet, but Edith came in here this morning to make sure everything was good. I hate to talk about folks, especially in the house of the Lord...but Edith is slow so you might want to check behind her. I have to get some cables from my car. I'll be right back." He said.

"Everything is probably good." I replied. We walked out together. I went into the bathroom and when he was out of eyesight, I slipped back in the media room, switched the video, and then went back to the choir room.

The choir sang their hearts out and Edith's solo brought the house down - there was not a dry eye in the building. Bishop Columbus' message on forgiveness convicted me. When he said, "Colossians 3:13 NIV tells us to **'Bear with each other and forgive one another if any of you has a grievance against someone. Forgive as the Lord forgave you,' I had a change of heart. The Scripture that got me was** Ephesians 4:31-32 NIV: **"Get rid of all bitterness, rage and anger, brawling and slander, along with every form of malice. Be kind and compassionate to one another, forgiving each other, just as in Christ God forgave you." Bishop Columbus explained that sometimes we have to forgive others over and over because according to Matthew 18:22, "Then Peter came to Jesus and asked, 'Lord, how many times shall I forgive my brother or sister who sins against me? Up to seven times?' Jesus answered, "I tell you, not seven times, but seventy-seven times.'** Forgiveness is not for them - it is for us. When we hold on to grudges we are giving that person control over our emotions. A lot of times we are up at night hating folks and worrying about them and they ain't thinking about us...Amen, somebody," Bishop Columbus said.

He was right - Aubrey controlled my emotions and my actions. This was not the way to handle our breakup and I did force her hand. I had become clingy. I was afraid that I would lose.

"Stop giving people the key to your emotions. Stop letting others' opinions of you make you feel less than you are. You are a child of God. You are enough just the way you are," the Bishop added. I was sitting here about to destroy my childhood friend. I didn't blame her from distancing herself from me. I had turned into a stalker. I tried to control her emotionally. "I don't know who I am talking to but somebody needs to hear these words. Before we do altar call and the benediction we are going to show a video. I was told that a lot of folks want to wish Bishop Joseph a happy anniversary. Before we roll the video I want to leave you with this thought. It is time that you walk into the fullness of who you are. If you don't remember anything that I said today, I want you to remember this: 'Greater is he that is in me than is in this world.'"

Oh God, the video! I got up, left the choir stand, and ran towards the media room to switch the video back. By the time I got there it was too late. I heard my voice saying, "First Lady Aubrey Joseph was my lover. She is a liar, adulteress, and thief. She stole $300,000 from the church's benevolence fund." I hung my head and walked to my car.

ALEXIS

As QUICKLY AS THE STORM started it died. True to his word Jason made everything go away. I know he knew people in high places; I didn't think he had that type of clout, though. To say I was grateful was putting it mildly. My main concern was my sisters and them not being caught up in my mess, and most important, them staying out of jail. The apartment complex was paid for, so we only had to pay the property tax.

I paid Aubrey back the money that she stole - borrowed - from the church and officially shut SC Unite down. The women still lived in their units and their sponsors continued to pay their living expenses, so we were still making money on the rent.

Lately, I had been spending a lot of time with Jason. Again, I went against my "I'm not getting involved with married men again" mantra. He was not at the birth of his first and only child because he's married, a political figure, and the baby is by his side chick.

Shamika had a lot of nerve to call Autumn. When she was burning bridges she didn't think that she would need anyone but Jason. I felt sorry for her. She only wanted true love and a family, which is what most women want. Her way of going about it was wrong. Like my grandmother used to say, "You live and you learn."

By the time I arrived at the hospital Shamika was being discharged. Autumn and Shamika's mother was there. Ms. Jean Ann was a lovely woman; she was about a foot shorter than Shamika, but you could tell where Shamika got her looks. Her mom was a little lighter than her. Ms. Jean Ann had more curves than her daughter and she was not a label whore like her daughter. She wore a pair of blue jeans and a plain white blouse with ruffles and a pair of flat slippers.

Sia was beautiful. She had Shamika's slim nose and Jason's eyes, she is going to be a doll. I helped them pack up everything, including the gifts I bought for the new mommy and baby. She had so many gifts and flowers that we had to put some of them in Autumn's car. As soon as I got in my car I called Jason. He answered so fast I don't think the phone even rang.

"Hello?"

"Hey, Jay."

"What's up, Lex?"

"I'm just leaving the hospital. Your daughter is beautiful."

"I know...Mika has sent me hundreds of pictures."

"When are you going to see your baby? I understand you felt you couldn't go to the hospital because of your marital status, but get your ass over to that little girl's apartment and see your baby, today!"

"Wow, you campaigning for Shamika?"

"No...I...she just looks so sad. Although her mom is with her I know she would want you there, too. So do the right thing, Jay."

"I just spoke to her and I am headed over there now."

"Great!"

"I want to see you tonight."

"Aren't you getting ready to go spend time with your newborn daughter?"

"Yes, I am not spending the night. I'm going to be over there for a couple of hours and then I'm out."

"What about your wife?"

"Damn...what about her?"

"Don't you have to go home?"

"When I get home I'll be home. Why are you asking me all these questions? If you don't want to get up with me just say so instead of playing fifty questions."

"It's not that, Jay; you got a wife, a baby momma, and you trying to have a girlfriend. You are doing too much."

"You don't want to see me, Lex?"

"Look, do like the old folks used to say...get your house in order," I joked.

"Right, right, you right. I got to get my shit together so we can be together. I love you, Alexis, and I'm going to make you my woman." I was silent. "Damn, the cat got your tongue," he laughed. "I have never heard you this quiet. I wish I could see your face right now," he joked. I still didn't say anything. I didn't know what to say. I had strong feelings for him; I was in strong like with him. I was not about to tell another married man that I loved him. "You don't have to say anything, I understand. Just marinate on what I said and I will talk to you later, beautiful lady." He hung up.

AUBREY

I NOW UNDERSTAND WHAT MY mother meant when she said "A liar will get you killed." I closed my eyes and took long, deep breaths in an attempt to control the pounding palpitations in my chest. My mind replayed the situation at church today like it was on auto-loop. My muscles stiffened as I suppressed the desire to flee. So I did what I always do when I have a lot on my mind: clean. Cleaning is therapeutic; it soothed me and time usually seemed to fly, but not this time. Time seemed to stand still as I waited in the kitchen for Kai to arrive. The kitchen is where we always have important talks, so I knew this is where it would go down.

The sound of the motor opening the garage did not stop me from rubbing the same spot on the cream and brown marble countertop. I heard his footsteps. I could feel the warmth of his breath. I knew he was watching me, but I refused to look up. Staring at the imaginary spot on the countertop, I whispered, "I guess you want a divorce?"

"Divorce is an understatement!" he yelled. I refused to look at him. He had every right to be mad about me stealing the church money, but as far as cheating he's a damn hypocrite; he is the one who came home with an outside child. I underestimated Vanessa's trifling ass. As God is my witness I will make her suffer. Somehow she found out about the money I transferred from the church account and gave to Alexis. This bitch used Kai's church anniversary celebration to reveal our affair, which had been over for months. The media ministry was supposed to play a video of people wishing Kai a happy anniversary; however, Vanessa switched the video and instead it was a video of me and her in intimate situations. I guess a woman scorned will do anything, especially when they are crazy in love.

I was tired of living a lie, tired of trying to be someone I'm not, and tired of spending money on a psychiatrist. I am relieved it came out. I hate Vanessa revealed our affair in front of the whole congregation. I would have respected her more if she would have just called Kai or emailed him, but to embarrass him in front of all them damn church folks - they would be talking about this day for decades. I could still see the look on my mother's face; she looked like she swallowed a handful of sour grapes.

My father, as usual, said nothing. He walked up to me, took my hand, walked me to my car, and gave me a kiss on the cheek. Before he left he said, "You are my child and I love you. I am here for you. Bre Bear, stop living your life for others and do what makes you happy. Now go get yourself together. Don't worry about KJ. Your mom and I will pick him up from the church nursery and take him home." He started walking away, but then turned around and said, "If that nigga puts his hands on you, you call me. I promise you I'll put him six feet under."

Kai stopped my hand from scrubbing and said, "Look at me, Bre." I stopped rubbing the spot on the countertop. It was time for me to put my big-girl panties on and face the music. It pained my heart to see the look in his eyes and know that I was the source of his pain. He spoke first. "Why did you do this?" he asked.

"I never intended for you to find out and I haven't been involved with Vanessa for months. I took the money from the church because I needed it and I paid it back, every dime; you can check the bank statement." After the fallout with SC Unite, I paid the church back with money from a savings account that I had in the Grand Cayman Islands. At least that part of the video was a lie. Vanessa's over-sensitive ass is making me rethink being a full-out lesbian.

"I am not talking about the money, Bre. I am talking about your relationship with a woman."

"I have always been bisexual, Kai...I thought if I married you my feelings for women would go away, and they did for a while. I was living my life for everyone but Aubrey."

"Did you go back to sleeping with women because of your dissatisfaction with me in the bedroom? Please be truthful. I know that after I got saved and became a bishop our sex life changed drastically. If I had something to do with it, then I apologize."

"I can't blame you for my actions. No, I was not satisfied with our sex life and I used it as an excuse at first. I saw a therapist. I have tried everything to get rid of these feelings I have for women, but the shit won't go away. I am gay and I want to live my life for me now."

"So I guess this is the end?"

"I guess so...I hate that all this came out at church. I never wanted you to find out like this. I will always love you."

"I am not worried about the congregation. We all have skeletons. Just wait until they find out about Kia. I will definitely be ostracized. We went from being the perfect couple to the scandalous couple," Kai joked.

"True," I laughed. We hugged each other, which is something we hadn't done in months and it felt good. I knew that we would be good friends and parents Kai Jr.

JASON

THE FIRST TIME I LAID eyes on my baby girl, I was in love. This was a love like no other. I understand; when my boys became fathers to little girls they all said the same thing - that she stole their heart. My little princess was beautiful. She was going to be a heartbreaker, just like her mother. I am going to have to buy a gun.

I was stretched out on the brown and tan leather sofa in our home theater room watching a taped recording of "The Voice" when Marian came home carrying a lot of department store bags. "Hello," she said.

"Hey," I responded. She sat down next to my feet. I had to move them to keep her from sitting on them.

"Can we talk?"

"I'm trying to catch up on 'The Voice.' This is my time to just chill and relax. Can it wait until morning?"

"No, it can't wait."

I sighed, sat up, and turned the TV off and said, "Talk."

"Why do you hate me?"

"Don't start that shit, Marian, or else this conversation is over."

"We used to be so in love. I know after the problems with trying to have a child I changed...became withdrawn and..."

"And you checked out of the marriage! I couldn't touch you! You showed no signs of affection!" It was like a dam burst and I was enraged. "All you cared about was my political career and looking good for your folks. You didn't want to hear about my other dreams or aspirations."

"That is not fair, Jason; I am estranged from my family because I stood by your side," she yelled.

"I didn't ask you to do that!"

"I know you didn't. I did it because I loved...love you."

"I could have been happy not being in politics. I could have been happy as a civil rights lawyer, giving back to the community and painting. But no, that was beneath your idea for a husband. You never respected things that I was interested in or what was important to me." I got up from the sofa and walked to the bar and poured a shot of tequila.

Marian walked over and stood next to me and said, "We can turn it around. If you don't want to be in politics, then quit. We can adopt a child and be happy again."

I almost choked on my second shot of tequila when she said adopt. "Adopt? I told you a few weeks we are not adopting a child!"

"The reason I brought it up again, I know a young woman who had a baby and she can't take care of the baby by herself, and she is willing to give the baby to us because we can provide a good home."

"We ain't adopting no damn baby. Yes, we can provide the baby a home filled with expensive furniture and we can provide the baby expensive clothes and a fancy education. What we can't provide is a home filled with love. What part of a baby is not going to fix us don't you understand?" Tears streamed down her face as she listened intently to what I said. I got a beer from the mini refrigerator under the bar and sat on the barstool. It was time for me to get my house in order and I had to start by telling the truth. "Marian, I have something to tell you."

"What is it that you have to say?"

"I have...I have a two-week-old daughter," I stammered.

She stood very still. "I know," she replied. I didn't say anything. I just waited for her to finish. "I have your baby."

"You have my what?! Where in the hell is my baby girl?!" I yelled. She didn't say a word. She strolled out of the room. I was right on her heels, yelling, "Where is my daughter?" She didn't say a word; she just kept walking. I followed her upstairs to the living room and there my baby was, asleep in her car seat. She squirmed as I picked her up and held her close to my chest. "Where did you get her from? Where is her mother? Where is Shamika?"

"She said she couldn't take care of her and asked me to keep her. She wanted her to be with her father."

"That's bullshit, Marian! I pay child support. I paid the rent for a year on her apartment and the car she has is paid for...I'm going to ask you one more time. Where is her mother?" She looked at me indifferently. I put Sia back in her car-seat and wrapped her pink receiving blanket around her. I turned around and grabbed Marian by her shoulders and shook her. "Where is Shamika?!"

"Where is Shamika? Is that all you have to say to me? You should be asking for my forgiveness for cheating on me again...for using my money to take care of your whore. I don't give a damn about Shamika. We are raising this baby together because ain't nobody leaving nobody!" She was pacing and talking to herself. She was rubbing her hand and acting very erratic. I reached into my pants pocket and dialed Shamika's number, but her phone went straight to voicemail. I grabbed the car-seat. I went upstairs to the master bedroom and slid my feet into a pair of black Birkenstocks, grabbed my wallet and keys to the Range Rover, and left the house.

Marian tried to stop me by barricading the front door with her body, and I pushed her out of the way. She fell to the ground as I opened the door and walked out. I didn't even take time to close the door. I strapped Sia's car seat on the passenger side of the back seat and sped out of the driveway towards Shamika's apartment. I kept calling her cell phone number but all I got was her voice mail service. My palms were sweating. I was filled with anxiety. I didn't know what to expect. From what I just witnessed of Marian's behavior there was no telling what she had done. When I arrived at Mika's apartment the door was wide open and the house had been ransacked. There was a trail of blood from the kitchen to the front door. I dialed 911 and then I called Alexis. Alexis and Autumn arrived shortly after the police.

"Who are you?" the police asked.

"We are her friends," they said.

"When was the last time either one of you saw Ms. Matthews?" Officer Taylor inquired.

"The last time I saw her was about two weeks ago when she was being released from the hospital," Alexis said.

"I saw her last Saturday. I stopped by to visit and watch Sia so she could get some rest and I talked to her yesterday. I told her that I would come by this weekend to help her with the baby," Autumn explained.

"Mr. Carey, you said you talked to her today...is that correct?" Officer Taylor said.

"Yes, that is correct. She called me when she returned from the doctor. Sia had her two-week checkup today. I told you this already. I also told you my wife brought the baby home this evening, so instead of questioning us, either get over to my house and question my wife or send the police over there." I was starting to get agitated with the little young ass cop.

"Calm down, Mr. Carey, we're just asking questions so we can establish a timeline. We already sent the police to your house." Sia started crying. I was still holding her car seat. I put the car seat down and took her out.

"Give me the baby," Alexis said. I looked at her; she looked so beautiful. "Do you have her diaper bag?"

"No...shit...I didn't see one."

"Officer, I need to feed the baby. Can I see if she has a bottle in the refrigerator?" Alexis asked.

"Ma'am, this is a crime scene. We can't have too many people walking all over the place," he responded. Alexis' eyes turned colors and I knew she was about to go off. Officer Davis went to the refrigerator and pulled out a bottle. "Here you go," he said.

"It needs to be warmed up," Autumn said, taking the bottle and walking towards the microwave. I looked at her and mouthed "Thank you."

"Mr. Carey, your wife has been picked up and she is at the police station being questioned," Officer Davis said.

"Thank you, officer. I need to get down there," I said more to myself than anyone else.

"We have to call Child Protective Services to come and get the baby," Officer Taylor said.

"No, you don't," I responded angrily.

"I'm sorry, sir, but we do until we can notify Ms. Matthews's closet relative to come get the baby."

"I am the baby's father, so I will keep my child," I said.

"Sir, we will need proof that you are the baby's father. I am sorry, but we have to do what is in the best interest of the child." Officer Taylor was going to be looking for a new job in the morning, cocky little bastard. I went to my truck and got the paternity test out of my briefcase and showed him the papers. "I am leaving so I can get to the precinct to see what my wife has done. And I am taking my child with me."

"Autumn and I will keep Sia until you are finished," Alexis said.

"Yes we will, you have enough to deal with right now. Don't worry - she will be in good hands," Autumn said. She walked into the baby's room and packed a diaper bag.

"Thanks, ladies. I will call you when I find out something."

"We will be at the office," Alexis said. I kissed my little princess and got in my truck. I prayed that Mika was all right, but I got a deep sensation in my gut that she wasn't.

SHAMIKA

IT WAS ABOUT 8:30 PM. I had just put Sia in her crib. After I bathed, fed, and put her to bed this was my time to clean the house and decompress before she woke up in a couple of hours to eat. I loved her so much, but I hadn't slept more than two hours since I brought her home from the hospital. I started running water in the kitchen sink to wash Sia's bottles when I heard the sound of my front door being kicked in. Two men entered with shotguns. All I knew was I had to protect my baby.

One intruder grabbed me before I could make it to the nursery. I started kicking and screaming with all my might. He body-slammed me to the ground and I felt waves of pain throughout my body. Everything became blurry. He slapped me in the face. I started swinging again and I was lucky enough to land a punch to his right jaw, but the punch didn't faze him. He slammed my head to the kitchen floor and put grey duct tape over my mouth. He tied my hands with rope. I heard Sia cry. I couldn't get to her. I was helpless. I saw the other man holding her.

I wiggled and fought in an attempt to free myself but it was no use. There was nothing I could do. Then I saw her - Debra from yoga class. She wasn't pregnant and she wanted my baby. She took Sia walked towards and said, "Don't worry, she will be raised by her father – Jason - and me, his wife." She pulled off her wig and it was Marian.

Debra was really Marian. All this time I had been talking to her in yoga class and she came to my baby shower. She had a good disguise; she didn't look anything like Marian. I saw pictures of Marian and Jason on Facebook. Tears streamed down my face as I watched Marian walk out of the house with my baby. When she left the two thugs picked me up and carried me out the house. I was still squirming and trying to get loose. I had to get free. My heart pulsated as they put me in the trunk of a car. I screamed but no one could hear me because they had duct tape over my mouth. I rolled as much as I could in the back of the trunk but I couldn't get loose. I started hyperventilating. I was claustrophobic. I was in full panic mode. In that moment I regretted leaving everything I had done.

I should have followed the rules and not gotten pregnant on purpose. I wasn't thinking, wanted Jason for myself. Alexis' words were true; I couldn't make someone else's family my family. I put too much trust in Jason, I believed he was not happy with Marian and the only reason he was staying was because of his political career. He lied.

I knew they were going to kill me and that woman was going to raise my baby. I would never see my baby again and she would never know her real mother.

MARIAN

WHEN I OPENED THE DOOR and saw the police, I knew they were there for me. "Officer, how can I help you?" I asked.

The officer asked, "Are you Marian Carey?"

"Yes, I am...how can I help you, Officer Smith, is it?"

"Yes, ma'am. I need you to come with me."

"What is this about? Am I under arrest?"

"We need to ask you some questions about Shamika Matthews."

"What about her?"

"Did you know her?"

"Yes, the little hussy had an affair with my husband and they have a love child."

"We just received a call from Atlanta Police Department. Your husband reported her missing. He's at her apartment and it looks like foul play." I just stared at him. My husband - damn traitor. I shouldn't have protected his image when I called the radio station. I should have ruined his ass, but no, I was trying to save his political career. How does he repay me? He pushed me to the floor and rushed to that bitch's house. I guess he thinks he is captain save a hoe.

"Officer Smith, am I under arrest? If not please get off my property."

"I'm sorry, Mrs. Carey, you will have to come to the station with us for questioning. You have the right to have a lawyer present during the questioning."

"Let me get purse so we can get this over with. I have things to do in the morning." Before I could get my purse another officer arrived and started whispering with Officer Smith. "Who are you?" I asked.

"I'm Officer Landon, ma'am." Officer Smith pulled me out of the house and put handcuffs on me.

"What the hell are you doing? You have to handcuff me to ask a few questions? I need my damn purse!"

"I'm sorry, Mrs. Carey, but you are under arrest."

"Arrest? For what?"

"Ma'am, you have the right to remain silent and anything..."

I interrupted. "Don't fucking read me no rights. Why am I being arrested?" I snapped.

"For conspiring and murder for hire of Shamika Matthews."

"This is a mistake. I will have your badge for this...do you know who my husband is?"

"Yes, we do. Please don't say anything else until we get you to the station and you have your lawyer present."

"This is a mistake!" I yelled.

"Ma'am, we have two witnesses who said that you hired them to beat, kidnap, and kill Shamika Matthews, and that you took her baby."

"Officers I don't know what you are talking about."

"Ma'am we have two suspects in custody who was arrested for robbing a gas station and they said you hired them to kill Shamika Matthews and told us where they dumped the body. We sent a car to the site to investigate."

I knew I shouldn't have hired them two clowns my cousin recommended. I wonder which one got nervous and started talking. I thought there was a hood code...snitches get stitches or some shit like that. I could feel my blood boil; my face felt flush and my hands started trembling.

At this point I had nothing to lose. Jason left and took my baby. I started ranting. "He disrespected me. We took vows. We were supposed to be together until death do us part. He is a traitor. First he cheated on me with some bitch he met at a brothel, and to add insult to injury he got his whore pregnant and had the audacity to take care of her and his little bastard child with my money. I was not going to sit by and let some bitch take my husband. All that I have been through with this Negro and all the other tramps that I ran off - that he took care of with my money. I deserve this baby and the life we were meant to have."

"Ma'am, please stop talking...let me read you your Miranda rights. You have the right to remain silent..."

"I told you, I don't give a damn about no Miranda rights. What about my rights?"

"We are trying to protect your rights, ma'am, but you keep talking. Now you have the right to remain..."

"I had her killed!" I yelled. "I watched them beat the shit out of her, I took her baby, and left." I continued ranting. "I should have been the one who had his baby. We tried for years to get pregnant. I had two miscarriages and he impregnates some young whore. Some young dumb gold-digger and then takes care of her with my money."

"Mrs. Carey, please stop talking until I have read you your rights."

"I don't give a damn about no rights. I was going to kill Jason's ass, too, but death would have been too good for him. I wanted him to suffer every day as he looked at his child and know that her real mother was dead. I wanted him to suffer and have to raise the baby with me." The officers were silent as we rode to the police station. Finally, the Officer Smith spoke.

"Well, since you waive your rights - did you kill Sia Thomas, too?"

"Who? I only had one person killed...that whore bag...Shamika!"

JEAN ANN

I GOT THE CALL I had been dreading ever since Mika move to Atlanta. She done went and got herself killed. I told her she wasn't living right. She was movin' too fast, always trying to get some money so she can drive some fancy car, wear fancy rags, and totin' all those expensive pocketbooks. She couldn't wait to move to the big city after she graduated from high school. I knew it wasn't a good idea for her to go to school in Atlanta. I remember when they used to kill children. I was afraid this would happen.

When Autumn called me I couldn't speak. I was numb at the thought that my baby was dead. I just had seen her at the hospital after the birth of the baby and I even stayed with her for a few days. She ain't have no life insurance policy. All the money she claimed to have, you think she'd have sense enough to get some life insurance. Ain't nobody got no money to bury nobody.

All these grown-ass folks walking around here like they ain't going to die. I don't know why folks won't get some life insurance because as sure as ya born, ya going to die. Hell, we just buried Henry last year; his black ass sold everything before he died. It's just pitiful how he done Linda. She was a fool for my brother-in-law; whatever he asked her to do like a fool she did it. When he died her name wasn't on nothing. Henry drove her crazy before he died. I guess she was in love; I don't want no love like that. Hell if I can't be the tablecloth I damn sure won't be the dishrag. Lawd, it ain't been a year since we buried Henry and now we got to scuffle up some money to bury this gal.

Just as I was hanging up the phone with Liza, I heard commotion coming from the front of the house. *Who is this in my front yard with all that racket?*

"Don't let the kingdom fall, God, hold it up til I leave."

My sister Gladys knows she can carry on always acting a fool. Her saved sanctified ass always walking around with olive oil talkin' bout this her holy oil - that oil ain't no mo' holier than she is. I sho' don't need her mess today. She just messy boots. I got to figure out how I'm going get this girl in the ground.

"What the hell you talking about, Gladys? Come on in this house fo' you pass out in this heat and don't grease up my screen door with all that oil!"

"Ain't nobody told me nothing - I had to hear about it on the news!"

"Ain't nobody told you what?"

"About Mika."

"I thought Liza called you. She was helping me make calls."

"I'm just full!"

Full of shit, is what I wanted to say but instead I said, "What are you talking about, Gladys?"

"I'm talking about these young chirren out here runnin' these streets and not living right. Sister, we got to stay in prayer for these chirren 'cause they ain't got no mother-wit sense."

"You sho' right about that, sister."

"How you holding up, sister?"

"I'm doing the best that I can under these circumstances. I'm waiting for Charles Ray to stop by. He said he had some money to put on the funeral."

"She was living in the big city and she ain't had no insurance? Mmmphh...mmmphh. Well, I ain't got no money. I had to bail Walter out of jail. He got into a fight with his friend girl."

"What he doing with a girl, you know his ass don't want no woman in the first place. Last time I saw him I told him to get what you like! And that ain't no damn woman. What happened? What he do?"

"He jumped on that gal 'cause she scratched him in the face, wouldn't give him his stuff, and told him to get his zesty ass off her property. Whatever the hell is zesty?"

"It mean he a sissy and he go with men...he's gay and afraid to come out of the closet. He need to kick the door open and come on out."

"Naw, Walter ain't gay he is a ho; he's been married twice and runs around with all those foreign women. I ain't neva seen him with a black woman."

"You neva will, Gladys; ever since he joined the Army and traveled to Germany he think he's an international lover. He's confused. Right fo' I put Charles Ray's ass out he called us at four thirty in the morning to tell us that he's gay. Charles Ray answered the phone and said, 'Man gone... that ain't no news I already knew. Who cares? As long as you don't try to get on me.'"

"What? When, Jean Ann? That's news to me. Lawd, hold up the kingdom."

"That's why he didn't tell you; you too holy for common folks."

"Mmmph...mmmph, ain't nobody told me nothing. I'm so hurt he call me when he get in trouble with the law, but keepin' secrets. I'm going to put him on the prayer list. Who cooked this chicken?"

"Charlene dropped it off about an hour ago."

"I'm not trying to toot my own horn, but my fried chicken is da bomb."

I wish Gladys would get somewhere and sit down. She know good hell well she ain't all that good of a cook. I guess she forgot that she brought potato salad to the cookout for the 4th of July and it had egg shells in it. The flies didn't even want none of that potato salad. She always acting like she don't know nothing; she know when Walter worked at the hospital he would wear all those tight-ass white scrubs to work every day. Folks could see the print of his peter. Had all the sissies who worked in the hospital following him around.

"Sista, you talk to Gwen?" Gladys asked.

"No, she told Liza she will be over this evening."

"I hope she don't bring that Peaches with her. I can't stand that triflin' bulldagger. She ain't nothing but a monkey with a wig on."

"Gladys! I can't believe that you called your sister that!"

"I don't know why; she knew I was seeing Lamont and she had the nerve to entice him."

"Girl, it take two to tangle, so don't go blaming her. You need to direct some of your hate to him, too."

"Oh, believe me I do! He had the nerve to call me trying to get back with me, but I told him I wouldn't take him back if he was the last man on earth. Hell, he can't unzip his pants for another woman and think he going to unzip them for me again! How you gone cheat and can't get your pee pee up?!"

"What?!"

"Yes, that bastard couldn't get it up! You know he has the sugar and it mess with his peter. It was dead as a dog. He used to wrap a string around it when he unzipped his pants for me."

"Sister, you are a mess. Come on in here and help me cook this food," I said. I'm hoping she will fry the chicken; that is the one thing she can cook.

"What you want me do?" Gladys asked while putting on the red apron.

"You can fry these chicken wings," I said. Gladys glanced at me while carrying the bowl of wings to the sink. When she raised her eyebrows and tilted her head to the left I knew she was getting ready to pry.

Slowly she said, "Not trying to be nosy and you can tell me none of my bizness if you want, but did the police say what happened to that gal?" I knew it was coming and I was surprised it took her so long to ask. I didn't want to say too much because she never retells the story the same way; she always adds something or leaves it off. So I said, "They still investigating," and started peeling the potatoes for the potato salad.

ALEXIS

I TURNED THE LIGHT OUT in my condo on my way out of the door for the last time. Too much had happened in Atlanta; it was time for me to move on. I was moving to Los Angeles. Although I had a special place in my heart for Jason, he had too much going on with Marian's trial and life as a single father. He was still my friend and I would offer as much support as I could. Last night we talked for hours and I told him, "I'm here if you need me."

"Thank you. I got to get my shit together and find out who I really am and what I want. I've resigned from politics and I'm moving to Birmingham. I'm opening my own law firm."

"Good for you! I am so happy that you will finally be doing something that you want to do. What about running for vice-president?"

"That was Marian's dream and I convinced myself that it was my dream, but it's not. I filed for divorce. My mother is moving to Birmingham to help me with Sia. I am finally free to do the things I want to do."

"I wish you all the best. I need to get myself together too, and if our paths cross again when we both have our houses in order who knows what might happen." I smiled and said, "Goodbye, Jay."

"Goodbye, Lexi." I pressed end on my cellphone and thought maybe in another lifetime we could have been good together.

What a year this has been. Aubrey and Kai are going through a divorce. I never knew my sister liked women. She had been living a lie for so long and now that the truth was out she was finally free. Her business is still thriving; gay people support their own. I hate it had to come out in church. I wish I could have seen Mommy Dearest's face; that would have been priceless. She still hasn't talked to me since the drama surrounding SC Unite. I would say that it don't trouble my spirit none, but it does. I wish we had a close daughter-and-mother relationship. I have resigned myself to the fact that it's probably not going to happen.

She had the nerve to tell Autumn not to follow me to California and when Autumn didn't change her mind, she said, "Don't let her get you in no mess. She ain't nothing but trouble with a capital T." My heart was heavy when Autumn repeated what she said. She's mad she can't control me. I think she's lost her hold on Aubrey, too. When she tried to pray the gay out of her, Bre finally stood up for herself. I had no idea that Aubrey was seeing a therapist because she blames herself for the death of our brother. I hate that she's carried around that guilt and pain all of these years.

I am proud that Autumn is finally going to follow her dreams of being an actress and also performing stand-up comedy. She has always been funny, so when she did an open mic I knew she had found her calling. The move will do her good; it will put some distance between her and Kevin. I'm proud that she is dealing with her PTSD - although she refuses to take medicine, she is back in therapy. I will be glad to have her and my niece in LA with me.

I met with the former ladies of Side Chicks Unite for the last time. I thought starting an organization to get revenge on cheating men was a great idea. It wasn't. It was created out of bitterness and hurt. When I walked in my office it felt bittersweet. All the ladies were there and they had planned a surprise going-away party for me. I was going to miss these ladies and I was happy for the women they had become; more importantly I was happy they honored of the rules of the organization. I hated that Sia and Shamika were killed and I know that it was because of the organization, yet I couldn't take all the responsibility for them not following the rules. What is sad is they were killed by the same people. Malik hired